The Fire Went Wild

The Fire
Went Wild
a novel

JORDAN NASSER

To all the people I wanted to kiss.

1

ME, TARZAN

"I'm pretty sure it's Tarzan's fault."

"Huh?" Luke's voice was muffled, his head was turned away and face down in the pillow next to mine. I was on my back with his strong left arm lying across my chest, pulling me close to him. I had been awake for a few minutes, but I liked to lie there looking at the ceiling, enjoying the few moments I took each morning to silently thank the universe before he woke up. He knew I watched him while he slept, but instead of thinking it was weird or strange or even cute, he didn't think of it at all. Luke just "was," while I put all of my efforts into overthinking and over analyzing. But that's just another reason why I loved him. In the end, it was our differences that had helped to pull us together.

"Tarzan," I said, a bit louder and clearer. "That's why I'm gay."

"Babe... what are you talking about?" He lifted his head from the pillow, turned to face me, then let it fall back down, his eyes barely open. It was the first day of a brand new year, and we had partied hard the night before at our favorite bar, the Firelight, with our friends Bammy, Kit and Tommy. Bammy brought along a new guy she had been dating named Michael. Kit and Shawn were there, and Tommy had Meredith by his side. It felt good. For the first time in a very long time, we were all "coupled" and everyone seemed to get along great. We stayed until well past 3:00 in the morning before we took a taxi home, but no matter what time I went to sleep, drunk or sober, I was always up by 9:00 the next morning. They say you start to wake up earlier and earlier as you age, but I'm not looking forward to waking up before the roosters.

"There was this Tarzan movie," I continued, "when I was a kid. *Tarzan, the Ape Man*, with Bo Derek. One night my dad and I had stayed up late playing a board game, Monopoly or Payday I think, and it came on cable. This was before my parents split up. Mom had long since taken her bubble bath and gone to bed. I guess my dad thought I was old enough, so he let me stay up and watch it with him. Bo's 'Jane' character pretty much spent the whole movie topless, but prepubescent me kept hoping that Tarzan's loincloth would flip up with the wind, or get torn off while he was wrestling with some huge jungle animal. I kept trying fruitlessly to catch a peek where there was no peek to catch. It was obviously a movie for men who loved women, but I couldn't have cared less about Bo's tits. The hormones surging through my body were preoccupied and mesmerized by Tarzan's rippling muscles, strong thighs and huge pecs, glistening with sweat. I felt lightheaded, to tell you the truth. I wanted him to come 'protect' me and keep me safe, even though I wasn't really sure I understood what I was asking for."

Luke was fully awake now, lying on his side, his crooked arm supporting his head and his blue eyes looking into mine. His mouth was bent into a slight curve and he was breathing softly, as if he was thinking far more than he was going to let me know with words. Before I could start speaking again, he surprised me and jumped out from under the covers. He straddled my body, grabbed both my hands and held my arms forcefully against the pillow behind my head. He leered at me wickedly as I let out a little gasp of delight, my eyebrows (among other things) rising to meet him.

"Me, Tarzan," he grunted, hovering above me, naked, as he slowly descended to kiss me on the lips, lightly at first, and then with increased passion and force. "You're *mine*."

■ ■ ■

"Holy shit, babe," I said, after our little romp, "that was amazing. I need to tell you my Tarzan stories more often."

"I'm just doing my best to keep you happy," he said, grinning. "I don't want to lose you, again."

"No chance of that," I assured him. "I promise."

Luke planted a kiss on my forehead and swung his legs over the edge of the bed. "I don't know how you can live on six hours of sleep. Shower?"

"I'll be there in a minute, babe," I said. "You take some private time." And he was off.

I heard the shower turn on and I took another moment to stare at the ceiling and wonder how all of this happened.

The last few weeks had been crazy, and even though we were totally on track now, the turmoil that led us to this point had definitely taken its emotional toll.

When I left New York, I wasn't just leaving my boyfriend David; I was trying to leave behind the me I had become after twelve years of struggling in and navigating around the city. It changes a person, and not always for the better. I had hoped that moving back to the South to my hometown of Parkville, Tennessee would help me find the "real me" again, or at least the me I wanted to be. What I didn't expect to happen, however, was Luke.

My friend Bammy is now the vice principal at our old high school and she helped me get a job there as a theatre teacher, but running into Luke Walcott, the high school football coach, was a shock that I wasn't prepared for. He was both my childhood enemy and object of lust, all rolled into one. Talk about a love/hate relationship. But Luke's good heart and charming personality eventually won me over, and enemies became friends, and eventually lovers. He wasn't prepared to come out, though, and I pushed too hard, too fast, and everything fell apart. When my ex-fiancé David reappeared from New York City, I was confused all over again, and it was simply too easy to fall back into my old ways. David was my old habit, and a bad one, at that.

I almost fell for him all over again, and just before I was ready to say goodbye to Parkville, Luke, my job and my friends, I found out that David had been cheating on me all along with our mutual friend, Marcos.

Thankfully, Luke was still there. And here, with me now. We'd acquired a few bumps and bruises along the way, and we still had a lot to learn about each other, but

I was committed to doing everything necessary to make sure that that man stayed right next to me. For good.

"Hey!" he called out from the shower. "Are you joining me in here or are you already tired of seeing me naked?"

"You're kidding, right? On my way, Coach!"

■ ■ ■

Luke and I were not in the best of shape after all that cheap champagne we had downed the night before. And what's the best way to cure a hangover, besides not drinking in the first place? Hair of the dog! Since it was the weekend, we decided to head downtown for brunch and a few more adult beverages at Saul's Sushi.

"How y'all doing today?" the hostess asked when we arrived. "Did y'all have a good New Year's?"

"We did," I answered, smiling. "Hanging with friends at the Firelight. We just need some recovery food, now."

"Well, we'll take care of y'all, sure enough. Just the two of you? Did y'all leave your girlfriends at home?" she asked. She chewed her gum and took a glance round the room, looking for an empty table.

I looked at Luke, unsure of what to say. I had spent so many of my early years covering for situations like these that it used to be second nature to make up a quick lie. But after twelve years of living in New York, I wasn't used to playing that game anymore. In that split second before I could even formulate the words, Luke beat me to it and spoke up.

"Nope. Just the two of us. No girlfriends. He's my boyfriend, actually," and he nodded his head in my direction. "Cute, isn't he?"

The hostess cocked her head and looked at us both, slowing down her gum chewing to a snail's pace. "*Oh. Geez,*" she muttered. Her face fell, but she quickly recovered. "Sorry. Y'all don't seem... I mean." She smiled, slightly uncomfortable. "Yes. He *is* cute." She bobbed her head and smiled affirmatively and started chewing at a normal speed, again.

With that she grabbed two menus, turned on her heels and directed us towards a two top along the right side wall. My heart began to pound a little faster as Luke reached down and held my hand in his. Did he really just do that?

"Here you go," and she handed us our menus. "Your waitress will be right over to get y'all some drinks and take your order. *Oh.* And by the way. *Y'all make a cute couple.* Happy New Year!" She half whispered that last part before she winked, spun around and headed back to her hostess stand.

"Well, I'll be, Luke Walcott. You do surprise me." He was still holding my hand across the table.

He pulled his hand back, removed his baseball cap and set it on the table. "Always happy to keep you on your toes, Derek," he said.

"You know, not everyone is going to be as accepting as her, right?" I said.

"I guess we'll just deal with it as it comes," he said, simple as that. "Now can we eat? I'm starving."

We ordered two bowls of matzah ball egg drop soup, some lox rolls and the corned beef egg rolls, as well as a pot of green tea. We devoured everything as soon as it arrived, plus an extra order of steamed brisket dumplings. Within minutes, those hangovers were yesterday's news.

"I don't wanna go back to school," I mumbled, petulantly. I put my chopsticks down and nodded for the waitress that it was okay to clear the table.

"Well, I'm ready to get back," Luke said. "Now that football season is over I can devote myself full time to the track team." I could see the excitement in his face. I have a sportsman on my hands, for sure.

"And I have to get a play together for the theatre arts club. Something non-musical, for the straight actors."

"*Straight* actors?" He looked at me quizzically. "You separate them by sexuality? In high school?"

"No! It's an expression. A term!" After he pointed it out, it did seem strange. "The 'straight' actors or dancers have one less talent than the hyphenate actor-dancers or the 'triple threat' actor-dancer-singers," I explained. "Anyway, I just need to pick a play. I'm thinking something from Tennessee Williams. I have to do my part for 'The Liberal Gay Agenda,' otherwise they'll revoke my membership card."

"Cool." He ignored my comment, as he often did when I veered "too gay," then clapped his hands together, signaling that he was ready to get going. "Waddya say we go home and crawl under the covers and watch some old movies for inspiration?"

"I like the sound of that," I said, smiling. We paid our bill, left the waitress a nice tip and stood up.

"Thanks, boys," the hostess said as we walked out. "Y'all have a good day. Happy New Year!"

Luke stepped towards the curb to the Jeep and unlocked the passenger door for me. Always the gentleman. "Hey, isn't that Tommy?" he said, looking up the street.

Tommy and Meredith were walking slowly down the sidewalk towards us, holding hands. They looked up and waved, smiling.

"Oh, man, did we miss you guys?" Tommy asked, reaching over to give me a one armed hug. "We didn't want to interrupt your first New Year's Day together. Kit and Shawn are on their way to meet us for brunch."

"Get the brisket dumplings," said Luke, patting his full stomach. "Awesome."

"Will do." Tommy smiled. "Meredith and I are going over to the art gallery to check things out later, if you want to meet up?"

Meredith owned an art gallery and performance space downtown, not far from Saul's and only a short walk from Tommy's place. I'd say it was just a matter of time before they made it official and she moved in.

"It's getting to be a little more work than I intended," she said, hands stuffed in her green wool coat to keep them warm. "I'm gonna need to find some extra help soon. We were just going to brainstorm ideas with Kit and Shawn."

"Oh, cool," I said. "Kit's the most creative woman I know. I'm sure she'll come up with something. We're just heading home. Black and white movies and a lazy day cuddle on the couch. Maybe a grilled cheese sandwich. We'll catch y'all later, though? Enjoy your brunch! And thanks for last night! We had a great time."

We hugged our goodbyes and hopped into the car. Luke pulled away from the curb and started heading towards his house.

"*Oof.* I'm stuffed," I said. "I'm ready to pass out on the couch."

"Really?" He smiled at me, and I could see the mischief in his eyes. "I was thinking about what you said this morning. You know, I have an old pair of running shorts I could tear up. Maybe they could pass as a loincloth? That is, if you're interested?"

It's a good thing it was cold and the windows were up, because the Tarzan yell that came out of his mouth next would have startled any drivers passing by.

Me? I loved it. Bring it on, Tarzan!

2

WHISPERS IN THE WIND

Christmas break was over before we knew it. Luke and I had been pretty much inseparable since we reconnected, so I thought I should spend a bit of quality time with Mom and Uncle Barry before the first day of school. I didn't want them to think I was ignoring them.

"Honey?" Mom called up the stairs to me as I was running around, trying to get ready for my first day. I'd spent so little time at home, lately, that being in my old room was actually kind of fun. I was running through my typical "what do I wear?" challenge, with different outfits laid out on the bed.

"Are you eating breakfast with us?" she asked. "Barry wants egg whites. Any requests from you?"

"Anything!" I yelled back. "Be down in a minute!"

I went for the standard Southern conservative uniform: chinos and a button down, but instead of loafers I reached for my beat up checkerboard Vans. Always the rebel.

Mom was in the kitchen in her familiar pink bathrobe making egg white omelettes. I gave her a kiss on the cheek, grabbed the two finished plates, added a few slices of cantaloupe to each and walked into the dining room with them. Barry was already sitting at the table in his dressing gown, reading the *Parkville Post* and drinking his coffee.

"Good morning, Uncle Barry," I said, as I set the breakfast plate before him.

He put his paper down and pushed his reading glasses further up his nose. "Hello, Dolly. How'd you sleep?" he asked, then leaned in and followed up in a whispered voice. "You haven't been home in forever, so I assume things are going well with your beau?" He winked at me, and I just nodded.

"All good," I answered, smiling. "What's up with the egg whites? You're a grits and bacon kind of guy."

"Sequins, darling. They magnify everything. I'm about to pop out of my favorite frock if I don't get this ass under control. I can't take the seams out any further. It's egg whites, cottage cheese and low carbs for the foreseeable future."

"And no alcohol, of course," I said, mockingly, as I picked up my fork.

"I'm trying to lose weight, not kill myself, Derek. No need for extremes."

Mom walked in with her plate and sat down. "What are y'all gabbing about? Anything in the paper?"

"Oh, just Mayor Tazewell at it, again," said Barry, changing the subject. He and Mom never talked about their private lives out loud. I still wasn't even sure what she knew about her own brother's other world, actually. "It seems the warning bells from the volunteer fire brigade woke him up at 3am. It was a false alarm, so he's trying to pass some ridiculous sound ordinance. That dog won't hunt. Pass that coffee, will ya, Audrey?"

"Isn't he a member of the Bears' Club?" I asked my uncle.

All I received in the way of a response was an extremely arched eyebrow. Don't ask, don't tell, right Derek? I should know better by now.

The Bears' Club was Parkville's oldest and most exclusive gentlemen's club, but I had recently discovered it was a haven for closeted homosexuals, cross dressers and the straight men who enjoyed their company. Uncle Barry was The Supreme Grizzly and star drag performer, also known as "Beret."

Mom handed me the coffee pot and I refilled Barry's cup while we continued eating and catching up. I wasn't nervous about starting the new semester, but I just wanted to get going, so I ate fast, cleared my plate and grabbed my bag.

"Have a good day, honey!" Mom yelled after me.

"Break a leg!" said Barry.

We'd had a mild winter, and there wasn't any snow to speak of, but it was a cold morning. I started up my trusty old car, Willie Nelson, nicknamed after the infamous "Honk if you love Willie Nelson" bumper sticker that Mom had placed there years ago. I set the radio to the local pop station to wake me up, and we were on the road again.

■ ■ ■

"Happy New Year, Miss Mabel. How was your holiday?" I asked as I walked into the first floor office of Parkville High School.

"You mean my *Christmas*?" she answered. "All you 'politically correct' bozos are afraid to say that word, isn't that right, Derek Walter?"

I just laughed to myself. Miss Mabel had been around for so long that things just went her way and no other. No one else had a fighting chance.

"My Christmas was the same as it always is," she continued, without even looking up from her computer, her reading glasses dangling on the tip of her nose. "I ate too much, people gave me useless gifts and I ended up with way too many fruit cakes. Bammy's back in her office waitin' for ya. She's asked me three times if you done come in yet. Do me a favor and get back there, pronto, before she asks me again? I got things to do."

"Yes, ma'am." I pushed past the swinging half-door and made my way down the hall.

"Caffeine, Miss Talbot?" I asked, leaning in to Bammy's office with a couple of to-go cups in hand.

"Derek! How did you know I needed coffee?" she said as she came out from around her desk to give me a hug.

"Uh, because you always do?" I smiled as I handed her a cup and took a seat opposite her desk.

"So, I haven't seen you since New Year's Eve," she started. "How's the happy couple? No regrets?"

"None, with Luke," I said. "He's amazing." I fidgeted a bit and took a deep breath. "But I really dodged a bullet with David, didn't I? Thanks for not telling me what an awful beast he was, but in the future, can you and Kit just pull me aside and be brutally honest with me, please? No more of this *we don't talk about it, we're polite Southerners* thing, okay? Because I know y'all had to be whispering some serious shit behind my back."

"All with love, Derek," she assured me, giggling, as she sat back down in her swivel chair. "All with love. I'm sorry. Really I am. We just couldn't. It seemed like you had made up your mind. And he *did* put on a pretty good show in public. We were just as convinced as you were. That whole *Sleeping with the Enemy* thing was a shocker, though." She raised her eyebrows and let out a small, uncomfortable laugh. "But that's all over. Movin' on!"

"And moving up," I said. "Tell me more about Michael? I liked him, actually. We didn't really talk about anything deep the other night. I was a little too busy hanging on to Luke. But he seems like a cool guy. What's his story? He said you two met at a school board meeting? Sounds sexy," I teased as I sipped my coffee.

"Oh, shut your mouth," she said. "Not all of us have hook up apps we can lean on."

"Jealous much?"

She didn't answer. Her gaze drifted towards the wall and back, like she was suddenly lost in thought. I hadn't seen her worked up over a guy in years, so I was enjoying this.

"Well," she started, "yes, I met him at the last school board meeting at the beginning of December. I didn't want to tell you, in case it didn't work out. The board hired him as an external financial advisor. Very 'sexy,' I know. There have been some problems with the budget in the last few quarters, and I guess we screwed up a few things, so we thought it best to bring in some outside help. Anyway, he walked in and I just, well, I just smiled. I could feel myself acting like a nervous girl, and that was strange to me. Normally, I just walk up to a guy I like, knock him right down and drag him off to a corner, but there was something sweet about him that made me feel girly, you know? Like I was soft. I couldn't take my eyes off him during his presentation, and when the meeting was over and I was grabbing my coat, he just tagged along and walked me to my car. The next thing I know, I said yes to a dinner date. I thought to myself, 'What am I doing?' This is a guy my mother would actually approve of!" she continued. "We went out to dinner, and he was such a gentleman. We really had a nice time. He told me about his life. He came from nothing, Derek. His mom was a single mother and she gave him up when he was a baby. He was raised in the foster care system, and he bounced around quite a bit as a kid, mainly in North Parkville."

North Parkville was the decidedly rougher part of town, where those of us who lived out west rarely ventured.

"Eventually, one family asked to keep him, and he was raised by an older couple whose child had died at birth. He was their 'replacement' kid, and he said he had a happy enough life. He worked at his foster parents' grocery store and saved his money and went to the University of Tennessee, like us, but I guess we all ran in different circles. Plus, he's a few years younger than we are, so we just missed him. But I'm glad he found me now." She smiled, brightly.

"Bammy," I said, reaching out for her hand, "I am so happy for you, my friend. I'm looking forward to getting to know him better. Why don't you bring him to the Firelight on Friday and we can all catch up without the New Year's hoopla? Unfortunately right now, I have to go prepare for my first classroom full of kids, so I need to run. Duty calls, right?"

"Tell me about it," she said. "Principal Bellman was rarely here last semester. Let's hope he decides to work a bit more this school year. I don't think I can run this show on my own."

"Oh, we know you can, Miss Talbot," I said. "We have faith in you."

■ ■ ■

Besides my Introduction to Acting and Advanced Acting classes, I also taught two Speech and Communications courses and held reign over a one-hour study hall. My planning period was scheduled after lunch, so if I was creative with my time, I could actually take a two hour break in the day before returning for my last class. That proved awfully convenient, considering I had the hots for the football/ track coach, and he just happened to be my secret boyfriend. Insert winking smiley emoticon here.

Luke and I had been pretty careful since his slow "coming out." Our close friends knew, of course, and his dad was working on coming around to the situation, but we were extremely careful at school. If I spent the night at his place, which was a few nights a week, we made sure to arrive separately, at staggered times. I usually made a coffee run in the morning, anyway. He spent most of his time at school down near the track field or the football stadium, while I was wandering around the liberal arts wing, so we didn't bump into each other as often as you would think. He did teach a health class on the main campus, but as you can imagine, it was quite a joke, so it didn't take up very much of his time.

When the sexual education segment of the syllabus was announced, in fact, a few parents threatened the school board, and as usual the board caved to their demands. So sex ed at Parkville High was reduced to a two day discussion in the final semester of a student's senior year health class. Freshmen, sophomores and juniors were barred from the discussion, and by the time students were seniors, most of them had already taken health, so very few kids were instructed in anything at all. And the closeted gay kids? Well, it was all pretty useless to them. Due to all the ridiculous compromises, basic anatomy was covered, but the topic of contraception (and homosexuality) was to be avoided at all costs, and the pro-abstinence lecture consisted of the following speech: "Hi kids. This is sex ed. Basically, don't do it. Any questions?" Following that, the teachers were instructed to go into excruciatingly gory details about every sexually transmitted disease known to man, as well as some that only prospered in the animal kingdom. The end.

Our paths did cross at lunch, however, so that was our time to catch up. We started meeting rather regularly, usually with Bammy, so we weren't just the two of us. We'd sit at the teachers' table in the lunchroom and trade stories about the students, our fellow teachers, local politics, sports, you name it.

Occasionally Luke and I would have lunch off campus, and I'd jump in his car and we'd take off, staying away well into my planning period. On warmer days we would go running at the lake, other days we would spend an hour and a half in his bedroom, fulfilling every last one of our fantasies. Let me tell you, he was getting really good at that Tarzan yell. Some days, we'd even have time for lunch! Kidding.

■ ■ ■

The first week of the new semester breezed by rather smoothly, without any major incidents. Luke pulled the Jeep into the school parking lot, and I reminded myself to pull my hand away from his knee. After so many years of being open and free in New York City, adjusting to playing this game of hiding and lying for Luke's sake had actually made me a bit nervous. We'd just gone for a run and a quick bite to eat during our lunch break, and we were a little winded, our cheeks rosy and pink from the exercise. As we walked towards the school, I noticed a group of students watching us while they were hanging out in front, getting a little winter sun.

"I'm not crazy, but they are definitely staring at us, right?" Luke said, trying to be casual as we surveyed the gawking kids. I didn't want to feed his growing paranoia, but in this case he was correct. However, a bit of calculated misdirection on my part felt like the better choice.

"Babe, you're hot as hell," I said, not lying. "If they're not staring at you, something's wrong with them."

"Lookin' good, Coach Walcott, Mr. Walter." Jett Winthrop gave a sly smirk and a nod of his forehead to Luke as we walked by them and headed towards the glass double door entrance. Surrounded by pretty girls and adoring hangers-on, Jett was a junior whose athletic star was on the rise at Parkville. He had it all: blond, good looks, a healthy bank account and a fancy car. Unfortunately, he was also a snarky little shit, and Luke had dated his mom, Amber, in high school.

"Cute couple," we heard him mumble under his breath, and the girls started to giggle.

Luke started to slow down his pace. I could see his body tense up. "*Luke*," I whispered. "*Keep walking. Do not feed that fire.*"

He clenched his jaw tight and pulled open the glass door, taking my advice and ignoring the words he had just heard.

Crap. Was it starting already? We had tried so hard to play it cool. Had someone told? Or did Jett just make a lucky guess?

■ ■ ■

I pulled Willie into Mom's driveway after school. Her car was parked in front of mine and the back door was wide open. There were a few bags of groceries remaining on the seat, so I grabbed the rest of them, shut the door and walked in the house. Mom was in the kitchen placing a paper grocery bag on the counter. She refused to get the plastic bags because you couldn't recycle them, and she could always figure out a second or third use for the paper ones. She considered it her part towards helping the environment. "*Ooh*, thanks, sweetie. Just set those up here and I'll put them away. How was school?" She brushed her hair away from her eyes and flashed me a smile.

"Hey, all good," I lied and gave her a quick kiss on the cheek. "What's up with all the groceries?"

"Well, it was double coupon day, plus I get my senior discount, so I went a little crazy. I got you a box of Little Debbie Snack Cakes. You used to love those."

I had to hold back my complaint. I didn't eat those things anymore, but she was doing her best and she loved me. It was just easier to say, "Thanks, Mom. Cool. What's for dinner?"

"Barry's cooking tonight," she said, warily. "He wants to put something on the grill. You know he's on this high protein, low carb thing. I can't figure it out. I just eat whatever, you know?"

We put away the rest of the groceries and then she stopped and just looked at me, as she often does when she's about to ask a serious question and she wants a straight answer.

"Now that that's done," she said, leaning back against the counter, "tell me the truth. What's going on? I had a funny feeling today, and I just need you to tell me I'm wrong."

I smiled, furrowed my brow and shook my head. There was no sense hiding anything from her. Mom had Spidey sense, and when it tingled, she was often right.

"It's really nothing to worry about," I said. "Things with Luke are great. I haven't heard a word from David, and I don't expect to. The only thing that could have possibly given you a funny feeling is the school. We are really going out of our way to keep our relationship under wraps, but I don't know how long we can keep it quiet, and I guess I'm a little worried about what will happen when it all comes out. Literally."

"Well, any fool can look at the two of you and see you're in love," she said.

My smile brightened. That made me happy, but it also made me take a deep breath.

"Yeah, probably," I said, nodding. "But let's hope that Southern sensibility kicks in and people just start looking the other way. Because if they don't, we're about to stir up a hornet's nest."

3

HAIL, HAIL, THE GANG'S ALL HERE

"Derek, honey, I'm gonna need some adult beverages, stat. And I'm talking an IV drip, if you catch my drift."

I stopped by Bammy's office on my way out the door on Friday afternoon. She was sitting at her desk looking like a hurricane had just departed the small confines of her grey-walled, educational prison cell. Bammy was a colored sticky-note kind of girl, and she stuck them everywhere: her planning calendar, her white board, her phone. She used them for reminders, notes and inspirational messages to herself, and there was a color coding system that only she could understand. I was surprised there wasn't one on her forehead written in reverse text so that she could read it when she went to the bathroom.

"What's the deal?" I asked, taking a seat in front of her desk. "My week went pretty well. Only a few situations that made me question every choice I have made in life up to this point," I joked. "Seriously, are you ok?"

She looked more flustered than I had ever seen her.

"It's Principal Bellman," she said. "He's here in body, but it's like talking to a revived corpse. At this point, I'm lucky he even shows up, but when he does, it's obvious he's just collecting a paycheck. The man has no fire, Derek. I'm at my wits' end."

Little did Bammy know I had seen Principal Bellman at his fiery best at the Bears' Club. I spotted him on stage one night when I was visiting Uncle Barry. Edward Bellman was better known as "Belle" at the club, and her specialty was boozy, brassy jazz numbers from the 1960s. Think Shirley Bassey, Dinah Washington and Nancy Wilson. The fact that these were all black singers was not lost on me. Race, however, was another topic we didn't discuss too loudly in the South.

"Well, let's make sure you have a fun night tonight, then," I said. "You're bringing Michael, right? How are things going with him?"

"Honestly? Frighteningly well," she said, and her eyes were practically dancing. "I've seen him a few times this week, and I tell ya, all the stress of the day just melts when he kisses me. Seriously, Derek, this guy can romance. He just lifts me off my feet, sometimes literally. I tell you, I was so wrong going after the weak guys all those years. I thought I wanted someone I could boss around. I got this whole 'strong Southern woman' thing from my mom, you know, so I avoided men with backbones. But this one? He may be physically stronger than me, but emotionally he's my equal... and I love it!"

"That sounds awesome," I said, smiling. I was relieved she had finally met a decent guy. "Have you met his parents yet? I guess it's too early, right?"

"Oh, totally," she agreed, shaking her head. "I want to make a good impression, so I'm trying to ask him the right questions before I meet them." Only Bammy would approach meeting the parents as something she needed to study for.

"They're his foster parents, remember," she continued, "but he was with them longer than any of his other homes. He even took their last name, Taylor. I get kinda sad when I hear his stories, actually. It just breaks my heart. I just imagine little Michael wondering why his real parents deserted him. But he clams up when I bring it up, so I've learned to keep my mouth shut on that one. And you know that is not easy for me, my friend."

"True story." I had to agree Bammy was not the kind of woman to keep quiet when she had something on her mind. Michael would discover that soon enough. "All right, Bammy, I'm outta here. Luke is swinging by the house to pick me up and I'm spending the weekend at his place. See you at the Firelight around 9 o'clock?"

"As long as you have that vodka IV ready, I'm there!"

■ ■ ■

I parked my car in the driveway, and it appeared I was the only one home. I walked in the door, placed my school stuff at the foot of the stairs, and meandered towards the kitchen to stare at the contents of the fridge and do my part to needlessly raise the electric bill. Mom's refrigerator was the same today as it was when I was growing up: filled with every condiment, jam and salad dressing known to man, but not a single thing to eat. Honestly, it felt like regression therapy, but that little flickering light inside was comforting, somehow. Didn't she just go to the store? The old telephone on the wall started ringing and brought me back to the present.

"Walter Summer Home," I said into the receiver. "Some are here, some are not. This is Derek your front desk clerk speaking. How may I direct your call?"

Silence, then a moment. "Hello?" I said. "Just kidding. This is Derek." I could hear someone breathing, and then they hung up.

Huh. No sense of humor. And Mom never invested in Caller ID, so I had no idea who it was. I probably scared the crap out of some call center sales jockey in the middle of the country.

I grabbed a Little Debbie (damn it, Audrey!) and sped upstairs to get ready for my man.

By the time I stepped out of the shower and packed my overnight bag, I could hear voices downstairs. I peeked out the upstairs window and saw Luke's car parked in the driveway, behind mine.

"He used to love playing dress up as a kid." Mom was standing on one side of the center island in the kitchen, while Luke was sitting across from her on a barstool. "I gave him all my old makeup to play with, too. He loved the powder blue eye shadow. Johnny, my husband, wasn't too happy about that. Whatever. He was just having fun. You know, come to think of it, I have some old pictures of when those girls down the street dressed him up once. Now where did I put those? Hold on, let me go get my albums."

"*Whoa!*" I shouted, as I basically threw myself down the stairs. "Let's not scare him away just yet, okay Mom?"

Luke stood up laughing and put his arm around my waist, kissing me lightly on the cheek. "Are you kidding me?" he said, pulling me closer to him. "I'm dying to see pics of you as a little kid. I'm sure you were adorable."

"Just the same," I said, "I'm sure we can do without that certain trip down memory lane. My early dress up days were not my finest work."

"Oh, don't be silly, honey," Mom said. "You were so cute in that old fake fur I had."

"Mom! Seriously?! I'm getting Luke out of here before you bring out old VCR tapes of school plays." I gave her a quick kiss on the cheek and gave Luke the *please can we go now* face.

"Fine, fine, I'll let you go this time. But Luke, you're welcome back anytime you want. You boys have fun, now." She reached over and gave him a big hug, then sent an air kiss in my direction. "See you Monday?"

"Yep, Monday after school," I said. "Oh, and I almost forgot. Someone called, but they hung up without leaving a message."

"Probably just a salesman," she said, nonplussed. "Did ya scare 'em away?"

"I did my best!"

"Good work!" She clapped her hands together once and we were off.

■ ■ ■

We swung by Luke's house first to drop off my bag and have dinner together. I was getting far more comfortable at his place, making myself at home. I had my space in his closet, my own drawers, my shelf in the medicine cabinet. Well, shelves, to be more precise. Luke's portion of the cabinet was basically toothpaste, deodorant and razor blades, while my side looked like the sample counter at a fancy skincare clinic. I hadn't crossed the line to Botox yet, but I was taking every precaution against the worst that gravity and aging had to offer.

Luke made his amazing chicken enchiladas. His housemaid/nanny Rosa cooked them for him and his sister Lana when he was a kid, and they did not disappoint. We ate our fill, took a quick shower and walked out to his car.

Luke held the passenger side door open for me. "After you, Mr. Walter."

"Why, thank you, Mr. Walcott."

I sometimes wondered if Mr. Darcy, or any of the other romantic heroes of Jane Austen's novels, would approve? Then again, at this moment I didn't really care.

■ ■ ■

We entered our favorite dive bar to the strains of The Smiths coming from the best jukebox on the planet. They used to have the old kind that played 45s, but the digital age wiped that away. First they switched to CDs, but now the songs were plucked from the ether, delivered by high speed Internet. Thanks, Al Gore! Regardless, they managed to keep the same musical vibe, without allowing the "wrong kind of music" to invade this secular space. Country and rock hits from the 1950s to the 70s mixed seamlessly with alternative music from the 80s and 90s.

Only the occasional current hit was allowed into this exclusive, magical playlist.

Our favorite circular booth in the corner was reaching maximum capacity. Kit and Shawn, Tommy and Meredith had pitchers full of beer in front of them, and they all stood up to welcome Luke and me. We like to hug in the South. A lot.

"Bammy and Michael are still at dinner, but she sent me a text to say we should start without them," I said to the group. "They'll be along later."

"Good to know," said Tommy, his arm around Meredith, "because this is our second round of pitchers, already." Tommy looked like he belonged in that booth. He was a relaxed, jeans and a t-shirt kind of guy, but I could see his girlfriend's influence creeping in. He looked good in a button down! Meredith, meanwhile, was always well put together. She preferred to treat every day like a dress up day, with flowery skirts and fancy shoes.

Luke poured us two beers from the communal fount. "Here's to friends, new and old," he said, and we all clinked pint glasses.

"So what's up, y'all?" I asked. Kit was looking mighty fidgety. "I can tell when Kit is up to something. There's a magic sparkle in your eyes tonight."

"Well, it just so happens you are right, mister." Kit looked sideways at Shawn, then over to Tommy and Meredith and gave a little smile. "I've been thinking a lot about my choices, lately, and seeing all of you so happy has made me put some things into perspective. I was an art history major in college, but I never did anything with it. Being a full time office temp pays well, but it isn't my dream. *I'm. Over. It.* And I know my boyfriend is a bit tired of hearing me moan about the endless parade of crazy bosses." She bumped shoulders with her beau and he gave her a supportive smile. "So, Shawn and I had lunch on New Year's Day with these two over at Saul's, and Meredith was talking about her gallery, and, well, I just got real caught up in ideas of how I could help, and..."

"We're going into business together!" Meredith burst out, as if she couldn't contain herself anymore. "Kit is going to be my new partner at the gallery!"

"That's awesome!" I said, reaching over to hug Kit. "Congratulations! So, what does this mean?"

"Well," Kit started, "I've been saving my money, and Meredith needed some help, and I feel like I haven't been able to do anything creative for so long. *Too. Long.* So, I'm investing in her, in *us*! And it's gonna rock!"

"I'm focusing on the business aspects," said Meredith, jumping in. "The books, the finances, the contracts. Kit will work with the gallery space, selling and coordinating the installations. Together we'll find new artists and book shows so that we have the best dang art gallery in Parkville."

"That sounds great, y'all," said Luke. "We're so happy for you both!"

My little Scooby Gang was really taking off. Coming home to the South hadn't been an easy transition, but so far, so good. Luke went to the bar to get us two new pitchers, and we sort of broke off into smaller conversations. Kit and Meredith were moving full steam ahead on ideas for the gallery, brainstorming creative ways to use the space and attract more clients and artists. Shawn was telling Tommy about his last gig at the Bongo Room. Some music scouts from Atlanta had been in the audience, and they asked him for a demo. Tommy had his plate full with some new private clients for his carpentry business. Luke was holding my hand under the table, playfully twisting our fingers and thumbs together, jumping into conversations when it felt right, but mostly he was just smiling contentedly. When Bammy and Michael walked in, they squeezed in next to Tommy and Meredith and joined the conversation, filling everyone in with their tales of work and local gossip. I could sense that there was something a little off with Bammy, but it didn't feel right to bring it up in front of everyone. She caught my eye and I thought I saw a fleeting moment when her permanent grin froze, but she caught herself before anyone else could notice. Always playing for her audience, that Bammy.

The sound of pool cues hitting their marks in the backroom cracked the air as Patsy Cline's "Walking After Midnight" came on the jukebox, so I made my move.

"May I have this dance, Miss Talbot?" I reached for Bammy's hand across the table, and she nodded graciously. Luke stood up to let me out, and she and I walked towards the jukebox, near the bathrooms. Romantic, right?

"Hey there," I said, pulling her in, "wanna tell me what's up?"

I held her in my arms, spinning softly to the beat of the music. Her head was on my shoulder and her hand was gripping mine tightly.

"Not really," she said into my chest. "It's no big deal. It wasn't a fight. Just an… impasse. I don't know. I guess I went too far."

"Well, fill me in. What'd you do?" I asked.

"Why do you think it was *my* fault?" She stopped dancing, lifting her head and momentarily looking me in the eyes. I raised one eyebrow and she just smirked. "Oh, shut that eyebrow down, Derek. Mr. Know-It-All."

"Ha!" I pulled her in again, leading her into a quick pirouette, her full skirt dancing about as we swayed to the music.

"I got nosy," she confessed, quietly. "I can't help myself! He's been so sweet, and I just want to know more about him. He's told me so much about the Taylors, his foster parents, I feel I already know them. But, then…"

"Yes?" We continued to move gently to the song.

"I asked about his birth mother." She looked up at me again, her brow creasing with regret. "I didn't think. I guess, I don't know. I didn't think about whether that would make him sad or anxious or upset or whatever. If it were me, I'd want to know. Wouldn't you? When you turn 18 you can request your birth records from the state. He said it was never important to him, and now, years later, here I am asking all these questions about these people who deserted him. I opened a can of worms, and now he's suddenly struggling with these feelings that he successfully avoided for years. I should have minded my own business. Frickin' Nancy Drew."

"Oh, Bammy," I assured her, "you didn't mean any harm. I'm sure he knows that. Everyone deals with personal things differently. You couldn't know how he would react. Trust me. I can tell he likes you. We can all see that. You two will get through this. It's just a bump."

"I know, I know." She lifted her head to look at me again, still worried. "But now I'm obsessed. I can't stop, Derek. My mind is just spinning. Think about it. His mother could have just been passing through town, but honestly, who the heck passes through Parkville and has a baby and then leaves? So, it must be someone we know, right? I mean, this town isn't that big. The odds are, we *know* Michael's birth mother. How can he *not* be curious?"

The jukebox switched over to a new song. We stopped dancing as I gave her a hug and looked over her shoulder at our table of friends. Damn it, Bammy. What sort of Pandora's box have you opened?

4

CAUGHT OUT THERE

Luke wanted to sleep in Saturday morning, but I woke up restless. Sometimes my brain doesn't shut off, and I was thinking too much about the night before and Bammy's revelation that we could know Michael's birth parents. I crawled out of bed, brushed my teeth and retrieved the local newspaper from the front porch. Luke had acquired a taste for a particular brand of Mexican coffee, thanks to Rosa, so I brewed a fresh pot hoping that the smell would wake him from his slumber. He went into full hibernation mode when he slept, while I on the other hand sawed logs that could wake the neighbors. He never complained.

The front page of the *Parkville Post* had a continuing story about Mayor Tazewell's latest crusade against the "spread of illicit establishments swarming over our town." He had a plan to enact strict zoning measures that would effectively close several legitimate businesses, including our favorite strip club/pizza parlor Chesty Cheese. I wondered if he realized that his own private refuge, the Bears'

Club, could be shuttered if it were more widely known what really went on inside? I think the Southern definition of hypocrisy somehow doesn't include the actions of the more conservative members of our society.

"*Ah*, my evil plan worked!" I looked over my paper to see Luke standing in the doorframe of the kitchen in his boxer shorts, rubbing the sleep from his eyes. "Coffee's on the counter." He mumbled a greeting, gave me a quick peck and walked over to grab his mug.

"Want to go for a run this morning?" I asked.

He stared at me blankly, then took two sips of coffee. "How the hell are you so chipper after all those drinks?" he practically whispered, taking a seat across from me.

"Practice," I answered. "Lots and lots of practice."

■ ■ ■

He parked the Jeep at his usual spot at the park. It wasn't very crowded this morning, but there were a few other cars there. "How 'bout we make this interesting," I said. "A little side bet?"

"Sure thing. What are the stakes?" he asked.

"If *I* win, you have to take me out for dinner tonight. If *you* win, I'll let you pick up the check." I grinned, hoping he was still slightly asleep.

"You'll *let* me? Interesting wager you've laid out there," he said. "But you can't slip anything past me, mister. Either way you phrase it, I win," he smirked.

We went twice around the lake, and I kept pace with him as best as I could, but he sped past me and beat me quite handily in the final stretch. He'd been training quite a bit after Christmas, gearing up for his spring stint as track coach. He was in great shape already, but when he pushed himself, he really saw fast results.

We were stretching after our run on a patch of grass near the asphalt, when a bright red Corvette pulled into the lot. I felt a knot in my stomach when the door opened and Jett Winthrop stepped out in his running gear. Awesome. Just who we needed to brighten our day.

"Well, well, well," he grinned, staring at the two of us. "Here we are, together again. Y'all are just thick as thieves, huh?"

"What's your point, Jett?" Luke wasn't in the mood to play, and I could feel it in his forceful tone.

"You know, Coach, I'm not so good at math," Jett started, "but it seems to me that two and two make…"

"Seems to *me*," Luke interrupted, "that you should be paying more attention to *yourself* and worrying a little less about other people. I wouldn't say your performance on the track was anything to brag about this week. If you want to keep your place on that team and you're here to run, I suggest you get to it."

Jett let loose a slow burning smile. "Yes, sir, Coach sir!" he barked out and mock saluted, walking past us as he headed towards the running path. Luke reached down to grab his keys from the ground and stormed towards his car, not even looking back to see if I was following. I turned my head to glance up the trail just as Jett swung around and winked at me, suggestively. Shit. He was damn lucky Luke didn't see that.

We rode back to the house in silence. This wasn't a time for me to solve our problems or find something funny to say. Luke was pissed, and I could feel he just needed some time to stew, but I knew it was only a matter of time before we would have to deal with this, together. He pulled into his driveway, unlocked the front door, marched down the hallway and slammed the bedroom door.

"So… does this mean dinner's off?" I said to no one, quietly sitting on the couch.

This was *not* good.

Luke snapped out of his fog later that afternoon. I could hear his bedroom door open before he stepped into the bathroom and took a long shower. I was in the front room catching up on some reading. I still hadn't chosen a play for the students, and auditions needed to take place soon if we were going to pull it off. I was leaning towards a classic Arthur Miller, and I had pretty much settled on *Death of a Salesman*.

"Hey, babe." I heard Luke's voice and I looked up to see him standing over me in a towel. "I won that bet fair and square, so I'm taking you out to dinner tonight," he said, in a mockingly stern tone. "Don't try and get out of it."

"I wouldn't dream of it," I said, putting my book down and smiling at him.

Jett may have surprised us in that battle, but I could see it in Luke's eyes. We were going to win the war.

■ ■ ■

As the "winner" of the bet, Luke got to choose the place, so we headed over to the Tater Tot for comfort food. We decided on a fried everything kind of night to erase the gloom and doom from earlier in the day. Plus, we had been training so much that I wasn't even worried about the carbs. We had a massive fried onion as an appetizer, then chicken fried steak with fried green tomatoes and fried potatoes. The gravy was pan fried from the drippings, so I guess that counted, as well.

We had been out around town together several times before, but other than that New Year's Day brunch at Saul's, we had almost always been part of a group. Tonight there was no Bammy, Kit or Tommy sitting with us, and if anyone were paying enough attention they would know we were together. As my mom had noted, any fool could see we were in love.

The waitress brought over our dessert, one massive slice of Mississippi mud pie for us to share. It was a huge plate of chocolate gooey goodness covered in marshmallow creme. I was looking forward to the sugar shock when I saw Luke's eyes freeze like a possum on a late night highway.

"Luke? Babe, are you okay?" I asked, putting my spoon down. He was staring at the door behind my head.

"Shit," was all he said, under his breath. "It gets better, right? That's what they say?"

"Luke!" I could practically hear her blond hair, diamond jewelry and oversized purse as I turned my head to see her walking towards us.

Holy shit. Not one, but two of them.

"Big brother, *where have you been?*" scolded Lana, as Luke stood up to kiss her on the cheek. "I asked Daddy and Rosa but they're just quiet as church mice. Said they didn't know anything and hadn't seen you in ages. *Lies.*

Lies. Lies." Her eyes got wider as she giggled, menacingly. "I had to stop over there last week to get Daddy to sign some paperwork on the lake house. You're a doll letting me have it without a fight, but you know it was Mama's wish, since you're getting the big house, anyway. It's just easier taking care of all that now, you know, before that whole tax thing gets ugly. I'm sure you understand."

Yes. He understood. And *well*. Luke had mentioned that Lana was trying her damnedest to get her claws on anything and everything she could before their father, Red, passed away. He was still in great health, but she obviously didn't want to take any chances.

Lana Walcott was tall, blonde, and a (metaphorical) killer. Razor thin, she had been a head cheerleader in high school, and she rode her older brother's popular coattails as far as she could. Even farther, some would argue. Her hair was usually in a high ponytail or a low knot, depending on the choice of headwear (visor or headband), and she was always dressed in the latest conservatively approved ensemble from Talbots or J. Crew. The final accessories were diamonds or pearls. Any other gem was considered too flashy.

Following close behind, and eyeing us with a combination of suspicion, loathing and malice, all coated in a sugary sweet smile, was Lana's shadow and best friend since high school, Amber Winthrop. Otherwise known as Jett's mom, and… Luke's former high school flame. When it rains it pours, y'all.

Whereas Lana was all angles and hard edges, Amber was curvy and soft, a 1980's pinup brought to life, complete with hazy photo lens. Wild red hair led her to believe her own fiery fairy tales, and the moment she entered Parkville High she set her sights on Luke. Their romance was legendary. The jock and the cheerleader, always smiling and holding hands in the halls. "Mr. and Mrs. Parkville," for three years running. But even though she was pretty and popular and well liked, she lacked that laser focus. She wasn't as feared as Lana, so she ended up taking a back seat to her bestie, but together they were unstoppable and ruled the school, handily.

Amber and Luke dated throughout high school and were well on the road to marriage, but a few bumps in their first year of college quickly derailed that fantasy. While Luke was preoccupied with his studies and the gridiron, Amber was busy having the party of her life, and on (more than) one of those wild nights, she ended up in another man's bed. It took awhile for Luke to catch on, but once the whispers caught up to him, the romance was over and they went their separate ways. Amber ended up getting pregnant and marrying the guy, but that marriage didn't last long. Neither did the next one. Or the next. Throughout three marriages she chose to keep her maiden name, Winthrop, for herself and her son, as if she knew they were only temporary road stops to refill her bank account.

"Anyway," Lana continued, "I was just thinking about you and here you are! It's like fate. I just *love* that. Don't you?"

But Luke didn't love it. I could see it in his eyes. Small beads of sweat started gathering on his brow, and he began shifting uncomfortably in his seat. He flashed me a look of fear and I knew the problem, instantly. He had come out to Red and Rosa, but he hadn't had the conversation with his sister, yet. *Is this the kind of thing you want to do in the Tater Tot?* I didn't think so.

"Luke, honey, you are so quiet!" said Lana, continuing to ignore my very presence, as if she and Amber and Luke were the only ones in the room who mattered. "You haven't even said hello to Amber. *She's single again, by the way.*" Stage whispered singsong, followed by a wink. Unbelievable. Did Amber still have love in her eyes? I needed to act, and act fast, if I was going to rescue my boyfriend from this horrible nightmare. They say that bad things come in threes, but two was enough for me tonight.

"Luke," I interrupted. "Sorry, buddy, but we're going to need to get a move on if we're going to make that movie with the guys." Three heads slowly turned in unison and stared at me.

"The movie?" He looked confused. It took him a moment. "Oh! Yes, *the movie.* With *the guys.* Yeah. Uh, sorry, Lana, can we catch up later? I really need to talk to you about something, but it's gonna have to wait for another time." He folded his napkin and placed it on the table.

"Well, sure," she said, dejectedly. "But I haven't seen you in *ages*, and I'm sure Amber would just love to talk to you. Isn't that right, Amber?" Amber nodded and smiled seductively. "Are you sure you have to run? Now what's one little drink gonna hurt? You can meet up with those silly boys later, isn't that right?" Not getting an immediate response, her eyes wandered down to catch mine. "I don't believe we've met. Lana Walcott." Cold. Precise. She didn't extend her hand, as one should, but just stared down her nose at me and expected me to nod and agree with her wishes, like every other love-struck man who had fallen in her presence.

"Lana, this is Derek, my…" Luke stumbled.

"Co-worker," I said, filling in the blank and staring straight at him. "We both teach at the high school. Luke and I were in the same graduating class actually." I turned to look at her. "Derek Walter. You probably don't remember me."

"No," she answered, dully but with a smile. "Can't say that I do." Bored, she turned back to her brother and her smile lit up again. "Well, listen Luke, if you want to choose the guys over me, you just run along. I'm sure Amber and I can find plenty of trouble without you. Come along, Amber." And they walked towards the bar, purses swaying over their half extended arms, Tyrannosaurus Rex meets Prada.

"Babe, I…" Luke was stuck without words.

"It's okay," I reassured him. "Let's just get out of here. I just didn't think you could handle a scene in public like this."

"Thank you." He looked at me, apologetically. "Can we just go home, please?"

"Come on," I said. I needed to try and snap him out of this. "If we go home, we'll just crash. We need a little boost. I have just the thing."

■ ■ ■

He asked me to drive as we left the Tater Tot. He was dazed and confused, torn between wanting to tell his sister everything and wanting to just run away and hide. I knew he felt guilty about the way I jumped in as his "co-worker," but the way I looked at it was twofold: first, it was the truth, and second, it saved my man from a surefire public disaster. Coming out stories are best done in private and not in a busy restaurant filled with everyone you went to church with and all their kids. There's only so much that we can pretend doesn't exist in the South, but coming out of the closet with so many witnesses present is just crossing a line. He wasn't ready for a public flogging.

"Well, if it isn't my two favorite men!" Peaches greeted us at the door to Chesty Cheese, Parkville's very own combination strip joint and pizza parlor. "Y'all aren't normally here on a Saturday. To what do I owe the pleasure?" asked the proprietress. Her sleeveless silk romper showed off every asset of that stunning, ebony body that had the locals clamoring for more when she used to work the stage. Now that she owned the place, she just liked showing 'em what they could no longer have.

"Just a little life crisis, Peaches," I answered. "But nothing a few martinis and a pole can't cure."

"I like the way you boys think," she said, laughing. "Come on in and I'll hook y'all up."

We followed her inside and she led us right up front to the best table in the room. "Y'all don't mind sharing, do you?" and she winked at us and nodded at two people already enjoying the best view in the house.

It was Kit and Shawn! They jumped up and gave us both big hugs, and suddenly it felt like all that craziness at the Tater Tot was melting away.

"*Oh. My. God!*" cried Kit. "I love this! Martinis and my three favorite men. How lucky can a girl get?! Shawn didn't have a gig tonight, but we didn't think to call you. Sorry! Where have y'all been?" Kit was working a 70s theme tonight with a daring black pantsuit and a plunging neckline. She was rocking a turban and gold hoop earrings. Very Studio 54.

"Don't ask, don't tell," said Luke. He still looked defeated.

"You look amazing!" I said, eyeing her up and down, "but this one's had a rough night," and I pointed my thumb at my boyfriend. "I think he needs the Chesty Cheese VIP Package. I may even buy him a lap dance or three."

"Pass one over this way, if you're feeling generous!" said Shawn, laughing. Kit wrinkled her nose and poked him in the ribs.

Our friend Tammy was on stage performing. She had actually taken our advice and added sparklers to her routine. Girl was on fire. Literally! She eyeballed us and made her way across the stage, hopping off and ending up in Luke's lap. She took his hands and placed them firmly on her butt cheeks, shaking everything God gave her as she finished up her set to wild applause. To say she was the most popular girl in Chesty's was an understatement.

"Whew!" she exclaimed, as she swung her legs around and continued to sit on my boyfriend's lap. "That was fun, y'all! Where my singles at?" We laughed and helped her stack her money on the table. Kit threw in an extra twenty-dollar bill from her clutch purse, from all of us. Shawn held his arm around Kit, tightly. Who could ask for a better girlfriend?

"What are y'all celebrating tonight?" asked Tammy, stuffing her loot inside her bra.

"Freedom," I said. "Because there is no light behind a closed door."

"Well, I'll drink to that," she said, reaching over and sucking down one of our martinis. "But I kinda like those closed doors. A lot of these people are a hell of a lot more attractive in the dark!"

"*You. Were. Awesome!*" Kit smiled, clasping her hands together in front of her. She was like a little kid in a candy store at Chesty's.

"Thanks, sugar," said Tammy. "But speaking of closed doors, I love y'all, but I gotta run. There's a high roller in the Champagne Room, and his wallet has my name on it. Y'all have fun, now!" And she was off.

We ordered fresh pitchers of martinis and proceeded to tell Kit and Shawn about running into Lana and Amber at the Tater Tot. Basically, we all agreed that Luke and I had avoided a disaster, but in reality, we knew that we just postponed the inevitable. Luke had already taken baby steps out of the closet, and now it was up to him to decide when and where and how to continue that journey. I knew I couldn't push him. I understood that all too well, considering my putting pressure on him was how I lost him a few months ago. Now that I had him back, I was going to be as supportive as all get out.

We were enjoying our martinis when suddenly a piercing scream rang out in the air, and everyone jumped. Peaches ran into the main room from the front door with a double barrel shotgun in her hand and signaled for the DJ to stop the music.

"Hold up y'all," she yelled. "What's going on in here?" Everyone froze in place.

It was Tammy. She was standing by the entrance to the Champagne Room, black mascara tears streaming down her face, her chest heaving as she sobbed, gulping for air.

"Tammy! Girl, did he hurt you?" Peaches ran over to Tammy and placed a free hand on her shoulder. We were all shocked, unsure of what to do or how to react. "Cuz if he hurt you, I swear…"

"No." Tammy's voice was meek, soft, almost a whisper. "No. He didn't hurt me." Her lip trembled. "He… he can't. *He's dead.* Oh, Lord. Mayor Tazewell is dead!"

5

THE BELLE OF THE BALL

When the very conservative mayor of your small Southern town ends up dying in the local strip club/pizza parlor, word spreads fast.

The Parkville Police and the emergency response team showed up within minutes of each other. We were all told to stay put until they determined what to do with us. I guess we were all suspects or witnesses, depending on the cause of death.

Tammy was quite shaken up. Peaches had called in Tammy's boyfriend, Scooter, and the police allowed him to enter the crime scene, thankfully. I'm pretty sure she would have been more of mess without him, and they needed her to be calm enough to answer questions. (Sure, we shouldn't have all been in the same room when they questioned her, but hey, this was Parkville, after all.)

"Now, Tammy," the police detective said calmly, "I'm gonna ask you to just tell us what happened, from the beginning."

Scooter removed his camouflage trucker hat and handed Tammy a glass of water. Visibly shaking, she took a big gulp before handing it back to him. She was seated at a small circular table by the edge of the stage. Her fellow strippers had gathered at the pole behind her, while we, the audience, all sat quietly nearby, listening to her tale.

"Well," she started quietly, "it was just like my normal Saturday. Mayor Tazewell comes in pretty regular like, so I was expecting him. He comes in the back entrance and usually watches my 9 o'clock set from behind the curtain, so no one bothers him, you know? Then when I finish, I come off the stage and say hello to my friends and fans and what not, but I know he doesn't like to be kept waiting, so I hightail it back to the Champagne Room as quick as I can. He was there waiting for me tonight, as usual. He used to see another girl, Roberta, every Saturday, but since she retired he and I have been pretty much a steady thing. Well, not a 'thing.' Aw, heck. Y'all know what I mean. Scooter, honey, don't get upset with me. It's just work, baby."

Scooter smiled softly and held on to her hand a little tighter. "It's all right, Tammy," he said. "Just finish the story so we can get you out of here, now." It was his job to keep her focused.

"Right," she continued. "So, yeah. Like I said, he's been coming by every Saturday night for just over a year now. It's pretty much what you'd expect. He likes to see me dance, do some pole work. Nothing really kinky or anything, like some of those creepy guys who can wander in from the truck stop down the road. Just nice, like. Heck, he even chats about his wife, sometimes. They been having some problems, but who doesn't, right? Well, tonight wasn't anything different. I come off the pole and sat on his lap. We were having a glass of champagne. He always gets the good stuff, so I like that. He was talkin' about work, nothing I can really remember. Sayin' his wife was gettin' fed up with something or the other. She was tryin' to make him pass some new law. I wasn't really listening. I mean, I was smiling, just making him feel good, you know? Like, I was pretendin' to listen? That sounds bad, don't it? Anyway, like I said, I was on his lap, having a glass of champagne, when suddenly he looks at me with this kinda fear in his eyes. Like, he was sad. It all happened sorta quick, like. I was sittin' there, and he just kinda froze. His champagne glass fell out of his hand and it smashed on the floor, and that sorta snapped me back to reality, you know? He looked up at me and grabbed his heart, his chest, you know, like they do in the movies? And well, it all happened so fast, then. I jumped up and he just fell out of the chair and right onto the floor. And I'm standin' there just holding my champagne, lookin' down at him. I just didn't, I mean, I just didn't know what…"

She started sobbing again, and Scooter comforted her as best as he could. He put his arm around her and held her, gently.

"He was a good man, you know?" she said, finally, as she found her voice again. "He was always kind to me. Sweet. I wasn't too keen on his politics, but I didn't hold that against him. I was just doing my job." She looked up at the detective taking her statement, her eyes filling with tears.

The police seemed satisfied by her story, and they thanked her and told her she could go. We all started to get up, one by one and we each gave her a reassuring hug, as the emergency response team wheeled the mayor's body out through the crowd on a stretcher, covered in a white sheet.

Oh, how the mighty have fallen. But what a way to go.

■ ■ ■

I headed over to the high school office on Monday morning, looking for Bammy.

"Good morning, Miss Mabel," I said as I walked in, holding two cups of coffee.

"She ain't back there, Derek," she said, tapping away at her keyboard but not looking up, as usual. "Principal Bellman hauled her off for a meeting this morning. Said they won't be back till after lunch."

"So you *do* know where everybody is at all times, don't you?" I teased.

"I done told you," she said, "that ain't my job. But just 'cause it ain't, don't mean that I'm not interested. Now how 'bout you give me that extra coffee? Seems to me you won't be needing two, now."

I laughed and placed one of the coffees on her desk. "All right," I said, "I'll come find Bammy after lunch."

"I guess you got lots to catch up on, after the night you had," Mabel said, knowingly.

I slowed my step and turned to look at her from the door. "Miss Mabel, how'd you know I was at Chesty's?" I asked.

"Derek Walter, if you think there are many secrets left in this town that I *don't* know, you got a heckuva lot of surprises ahead." She reached into her desk to retrieve a small flask, the contents of which she quickly added to her cup, then banished to the back of the drawer again, with a flick of her bony wrist.

■ ■ ■

Bammy sent me a quick text after lunch. It was my planning period, and Luke and I weren't going for a run today. He and I had decided to play it as low key as possible this week, after our uncomfortable encounter with Jett at the lake.

"Behind the theatre. NOW!" the message said. Behind the theatre? We only went back there to sneak smokes when we were students. What on Earth could she be up to?

I rounded the corner, and sure enough, Bammy was inhaling a cigarette like her life depended on it. There was a newly opened pack in her free hand for back up.

"Seriously, Bammy? What the hell is up? Where were you this morning? I have major gossip, and I needed you!" I said.

She exhaled a huge cloud of smoke, and I suppressed a cough.

"Derek," she started, slowly and deliberately. "I'm gonna need you to start addressing me with a little more respect. You are looking at the *acting principal of Parkville High*!"

"Shut the front door!" I said. "What did I miss? Did Bellman die, too? Oh, my god? Was it a love triangle murder-suicide pact?"

"Honey, no!" she laughed. "You've been watching too much television. Parkville's fun, but not *that* fun. The community board met with Principal Bellman early this morning." She took another drag, and then exhaled. "They want him to run for mayor to replace Mayor Tazewell, due to his unfortunate passing. They need a 'family man,' a real pillar of the community. Someone solid, you know? So they picked Bellman. Which means..."

"You get promoted?" I answered. "You get promoted! Oh my god, that is fantastic! Is that why you are chain smoking? Bammy, you're going to be great. This school loves you!"

"Derek, I about peed my pants when he told me. Gosh, this isn't what I wanted. Or maybe it is? Heck, I don't know. But I said yes. I'm running with it!"

"So what does this mean, right now?" I asked. "When are they announcing it? I bet Miss Mabel already knows, right?" We laughed and I gave her a congratulatory hug.

"We're having a school assembly later today," she said, flicking the ashes of her cigarette on the ground. "Principal Bellman is stepping down, to run his campaign full time. Not that he does much here, but I think he's emotionally checked out already, anyway. They're gonna schedule an interim election for the mayor's office, but we all know that that is just a formality. There won't be anyone else on the ballot." Parkville was a decidedly one party town. "In the mean time, I have been appointed acting principal until Bellman is officially elected mayor. And then... that's it. I'm the principal! And a nice fat raise, too!"

"What did Michael say? Did you talk to him, yet?"

"Oh, he's thrilled for me!" she said, with a smile. "Now I'll have a bit more power with the school board, of course, so we'll be working even closer together. It's good that we have this thing in common, to work on. Because the personal life stuff has been a little tricky, lately."

"What do you mean?" I asked. "What did you do now, *acting principal Talbot*?"

"Oh, Derek," she said, furrowing her brow. "I stepped in it. But good." She put her cigarette out on the brick wall and placed the butt in her coat pocket. She coaxed a fresh one out of the pack, offered me one and I declined. I've never seen her as nervous as this before. Something major was up.

"He did it," she said, exhaling a fresh cloud of smoke. "He asked for the paperwork, about his birth mother. He submitted the forms and everything."

"Holy shit. And?"

"And… he won't tell me," she answered, looking down momentarily at her high heels, and then up again. "They sent him an envelope with all the information they had. I know he opened it. He knows, now. He knows who his birth parents are, but he doesn't want to tell me. He said it doesn't matter. It doesn't change anything. He said he's sorry he found out and wishes I hadn't pushed him to be so curious. He blames me. I feel like shit, Derek. What am I gonna do?"

"Bammy," I said, reassuringly, "this isn't your fault. Don't let him guilt you like this. We all have choices to make, and he made a choice on his own. Sure, you raised the idea, but you didn't force him. Just give him some time. Hopefully he'll open up to you, later."

"I sure hope so," she said, her eyes betraying how nervous she really was. "Because I really like him, Derek. I really do. And I just don't want him to be unhappy with me."

"Bammy, no one could be unhappy with you for long. You're an amazing person. We're all lucky to have you."

I gave her a hug and stared off past the parking lot and into the woods. When I made the choice to come home and reconnect with my family and friends, I was hoping for some simple, fun times. So far, there had been a little more drama than I had counted on, and I had a feeling it was just about to multiply.

■ ■ ■

The week was over before I knew it. On Friday after school I stopped at the grocery store to do some shopping, then drove over to Luke's place. I hadn't bothered texting him to touch base. Luke wasn't the text message type, whereas I could basically communicate with Kit through emoji, alone. Luke was more old school, and as I walked in the door with a bag of groceries, I spotted a handwritten sticky note on the refrigerator.

Derek - Off to Lana's. It's time I had that talk. Love you, L.

Yikes. I was proud of him and scared for him all at once.

I unpacked the groceries and started preparing a big pot of chili. I had planned on making a meatloaf, but instead I decided to make something that could sit on the stove, waiting. There was no telling if his conversation with his sister would be long and painful and drawn out, or shorter than a New York minute. Everyone's journey is different.

With the stove set to a slow simmer, I poured a massive glass of red wine and took my place on the couch, waiting patiently. I wanted to be here for him when he returned, ready to listen.

About an hour and a half later I heard Luke's car pull into the driveway. I quickly picked up the *Parkville Post* again so I could pretend to read the front page story about Mayor Tazewell's unfortunate passing for the umpteenth time. It was really all they could write about. Not much else happened here. I was nervous, but I was trying not to show it because I knew I needed to be supportive.

The doorknob turned and he walked in slowly, placing his keys on the hook by the front door. "Hey," he said quietly, as I eyed him over the top of the newspaper.

"Hey. Wanna go for a run?" I asked, trying to prove that I wasn't chomping at the bit to ask him a million questions.

He took his shoes off and lumbered towards the couch where I was sitting. He placed his head in my lap and snuggled in, under my outstretched arms that were holding the paper aloft.

"No, not really," he answered. "Did I miss anything interesting?"

"Oh, not much," I said, folding the paper and setting it down beside me. "We're expecting a cold weather front. That big furniture warehouse is going out of business, again. Third time, I think. And, oh yeah… the mayor had a heart attack last week and died in the arms of our friend Tammy, down at the local strip joint."

"So, pretty average day for Parkville, huh?" he joked. "Dinner smells good. Chili?" He looked up at me, backwards, from my lap.

"Yup." Those blue eyes of his. Every time I see them, I'm grateful.

He paused, knowing I was curious. "I don't want to talk about it, yet," he mumbled. "Can we eat first?"

I looked down at him in my lap and smiled, reassuringly. "Sure thing, babe. It's all ready. Let's go."

We ate our meal and caught up on the day, avoiding the "coming out to his sister" part. We gossiped about Bammy's promotion and how teachers at the school had reacted. It was strange enough that my close friend was the assistant principal, but now that she was going to be the big boss, I wondered if that would change our dynamic. Hopefully not.

We cleared the dishes, took quick showers and brushed our teeth: all the mundane things that couples do in a relationship. Sometimes I had to laugh at the fear and loathing that some people have of same gender couples in our society. Well, not laugh, so much. It made me sad. When it comes down to it, we aren't really all that different.

Luke and I crawled into bed and I gave him a peck on the cheek, then reached up for the lamp on the bedside table.

"You're being unnaturally patient," he said, before I could shut it off. I just smiled, without saying a word.

"Okay, okay," he sighed. "I've tortured you enough. We can talk about it now."

"Thank GOD!" I practically exploded. "It's been driving me crazy. You know I have no patience! And I was so worried about you. Tell me what happened! What did she say? How did you start? Did you cry? Did *she* cry? Are you guys all right? Did she pull that *oh, I already knew* crap that people always pull? Or even worse, did she ask 'when you knew,' as if there was this thunderbolt moment when you made that 'choice' to be who you naturally are, anyway?!"

"Slow down there, babe," he said. "Is this my story or yours?" He rearranged himself so he was facing me, in bed. "I just needed some time to process it all. I know it was killing you, but I appreciate it."

He took a deep breath.

"Well," he started, "in a word... it sucked. And it's all your fault."

But before I could say anything or make a face, he stopped me with a kiss.

"What was that for?" I asked.

"Because... when I got home after school today," he began, "you weren't here. I figured you were at the store buying groceries, or at your mom's house picking something up. Regardless, I wasn't worried, because I knew you would be back. And then it hit me. Hard. You were coming back to me, to this house, where we have started to build a life together. We've got a good thing going, and I can't share that with everyone. And suddenly, it all just felt so stupid to keep that hidden. It's good. *We* are good. And now that my dad knows and Rosa knows, well... I guess you could say I found my courage. Why the hell should I hide this from my sister, anymore? Or Amber? Or anyone? I love *you*, and I want them to know."

I gulped visibly, like a cartoon character. I was trying hard not to cry, because I wanted him to continue and not worry about me. But at this moment, I was so proud of him.

"So before I could change my mind, I wrote you a note and stuck it on the fridge. I called Lana and said I needed to talk to her about something important. I'm sure she assumed it had something to do with the inheritance, so she said to come over right away. When I got in my car, "Centerfield," by John Fogerty, was playing on the radio, and well, it was like someone played that song just for me at that moment. I needed that chorus to push me. When I got to her place we sat down at the kitchen table and she just started in on me right away, asking questions about Father's will and the lake house and all sorts of stuff that was just flying in one ear and out the other. I couldn't concentrate. I felt like I was about to change my mind and leave. And suddenly she just looked at me with a puzzled expression and asked me what was wrong with me. She realized that wasn't why I came over."

He held my hand, tighter. "I said to her 'Lana, you've got to know,' but she just looked at me funny, still not catching on. So, I figured it was best to start with a story, about when we were kids. I reminded her how we used to go skinny dipping down past our parents' lake house, with these other kids who lived down the road. His name was Bobby and I can't remember his younger sister's name right now. That's funny, but pretty telling. Anyway, we went almost every day that summer when I was twelve. Lana used to tease me, because even though she was younger than us, she could see that Bobby's sister was pretty, and she thought I only wanted to go swimming so I could see the girls naked. And I'm sure that was the main reason Bobby went, but the truth was, it was Bobby I wanted to see. He was one year older than me, and that difference in our ages was so small, but his body had matured faster and farther than mine and I couldn't help but pay attention to him. I remember staring at him in the sun and thinking how handsome he was, and even though I knew I wasn't supposed to think that, it felt right somehow."

I remembered those feelings, myself, but I didn't dare interrupt him. He was on a roll.

"So I told her about Bobby, and how I had developed feelings for him. Feelings I didn't act on, of course. But she looked at me like she still didn't get it. It's like she didn't *want* to get it. I thought of you, and I felt braver. So I told her that yes, I dated Amber in high school, and yes, we fooled around, and yes, I liked it… but there was always something missing, like I was just going through the motions, doing what was expected of me. At this point, she was just staring at me, quietly, almost daring me to go further. She looked angry, almost. I could feel that truthfully she just wanted me to shut up and walk out the door and never have this discussion again, but I had already gone too far. So then I just did it. I opened up, completely, like I did with Father and Rosa a few months ago. I told her I was gay and that I was in love, and that she had already met the person, and I wanted to share that with her. And then I told her about you."

At this point my tears were pretty much not a choice, they were a reality. Slowly streaming down my face, I wiped them to the side as he continued.

"And that's where it all went to hell. She said I'd embarrass myself, publicly. It's one thing to have a gay brother, but it's another thing to 'flaunt that lifestyle,' as she said. She asked if I've been to therapy. I said no, and I didn't think I needed it. I'm happy. She threatened to go to my father and tell him, so that I'll be cut out of the will. I told her to go ahead, that he already knew and that he was becoming more accepting of it day by day. That silenced her for a moment. Then, she really went mad. My sister. This woman who claims to love me, who I have known my whole life, she started saying these horrible things to me, about how I was ruining my life, about how I would embarrass her, embarrass the family. She asked me how could I do this to Amber? Like I owe Amber anything? She started talking about 'choices,' and how I could change. I didn't want to listen, anymore, so I told her I loved her, and I got up calmly and started walking towards the door. That's when she threw the fireball."

"Wait," I said. "There's something worse than hateful words from someone you love?"

"Much worse," he said. "Actions. She threatened to tell the school board I'm gay, to get me fired. To get *us* fired. She said that if we come out at school, she would make sure that the town rallies against us. She is threatening to ruin us, so we have no choice but to hide. She's backing us into a corner."

"Oh, really?" I said, tears gone, my adrenaline pumping. "Well, *bring it*, Lana. Do your worst. We have two things going for us, babe. First, we have each other, and we're a strong team. Second, my bestie just happens to be the new principal. What does she have?"

We were about to find out.

6

CCCP

"My boyfriend is an activist."

I placed my Bloody Mary back down on the table after having taken a healthy sip. Tommy was sitting next to me, and I was catching him up on the last week. Spring was showing its face early this year, so we were sitting outside on the patio at the Tater Tot on a Saturday afternoon in jeans and long sleeved t-shirts, watching the strange mix of downtown residents, tourists and panhandlers.

"PETA or Greenpeace?" he asked.

"The gays," I said. "Full stop. It took that man thirty years to come out of the closet, and just a few months to become Harvey Milk. He's an athlete, remember? He's just so damn competitive. He feels like he should win every time. Boy, is he gonna be surprised."

"So what's going on?" Tommy asked, pushing his sunglasses to the top of his head. "Family stuff? Work?"

"Both. And I'm nervous as hell," I admitted. Where's our server with our second round, I thought? I spun my head to take a look towards the bar.

"I already got it, man," said Tommy, noticing my Linda Blair impression. "They're on the way."

"You know me so well." We toasted with the last sip of spicy tomato vodka goodness as the waitress dropped off two fresh drinks at our table. Tommy's feet were propped up on the chair across from him and he had his face turned up, trying to get a bit of that early spring sun.

"So," I began, "it all started when we ran into Lana and Amber here at the Tater Tot last week. It was awkward, to say the least. I mean, those two hardly even noticed me, but Luke just about flipped. He looked a bit like a caged animal, unsure of what to protect or who to attack. I got him out of it by saying we had to run and meet 'the guys' for a movie."

"Man, that sucks," said Tommy, "having to lie like that."

"It's okay," I said. "I know he had a tough time telling his dad, and I just didn't think a restaurant was the best place to have it out with his sister. Anyway, yesterday he decided to tell her the truth, and… let's just say she wasn't as accepting as he hoped she would be."

"Ouch. Man, it must suck having to go through that over and over. Does it get easier?"

"Yeah," I said. "You should be so grateful you don't have to go through this crap. I mean, nobody requires you to stand up and say you're straight? How come *we* get all the fun?" I took another healthy gulp from my glass. "Anyway, he came out to his sister, and it wasn't pretty. She didn't go full on 'fire and brimstone' on him, but she came pretty close. She threatened to go to the school board to get us fired, so he's been super on edge this whole week, waiting for the floor to fall out from underneath him. He loves his job and he doesn't want to lose it. He's a great coach, and not only that, he's a *winning* coach, and you know how they'd hate to give that up. The funny thing is, she probably thought she was pushing him back *in* the closet, but in a way, she's actually pushing him *out* even faster than he had planned. I know him. He's not going to take this lying down. He's staying calm for now, but this morning he was talking about making a 'bold statement.' I mean, even I don't know if I'm ready to stage a love-in at the high school. I was pretty good with how things were."

"I mean honestly, what can they do?" asked Tommy. "It's not the 1960s. You guys can't get fired, right?"

"Well, actually we can. Gays and lesbians can get married now thanks to the Supreme Court ruling, but the anti-discrimination laws regarding the workplace are pretty fuzzy. For the most part, they don't exist. The few that have been put into place have been repealed. If we decide to actually come out publicly at school, or even worse, as a gay couple, then we're definitely second class citizens and there's no telling what would happen."

"Thanks for the civics lesson, teach," he chuckled. "But seriously, no wonder we have so many closet cases around here."

"Brother, the stories I could tell you. But I can't. They'd revoke my gay membership card. Enough about my problems, though. How are things with Meredith?"

"Just great, man," he said. "She and Kit are getting along like gangbusters down at the gallery. They found this guy who makes sculptures out of old rusted tractor metal. They're totally digging that. And they have a few new photographers they want to represent. All in all, they're doing pretty well."

"That sounds great! I'm happy they're making a go of it," I said. "This town needs every little bit of culture it can get its hands on."

"Tell me about it," he said. "Remember when we were in middle school and their idea of culture was to take us on a field trip to the dairy farm?"

"How could I forget? Some of those farmers were hunks," I laughed. I liked to try and shock Tommy by sharing these revelations, as we grew older.

"Dude, don't ruin my memories. We got free ice cream that day." He paused. "But that girl who handed them out at the end of the tour was hot, too."

"See?" I said, smiling. "Something for everyone. Cheers!"

■ ■ ■

I spent Sunday night at my mom's house. I didn't want to tempt fate by sleeping over at Luke's and then showing up with him at school. As I was walking out the door on Monday morning, the phone rang and I answered it. Another hang up. I made a mental note to myself to get Mom a more modern telephone with Caller ID, and at the very least get her on that Do Not Call list the government set up. Does that even work?

I stopped and picked up two coffees on the way to school, one for me and one for Bammy. She wasn't in her office when I popped in, so I gave the extra to Miss Mabel. She didn't even look up as I placed it on her desk. That woman saw what she wanted to and just ignored the rest. I was a bit jealous, if you want to know the truth. I spent most of my life worrying about things that held no consequence, and then tried to run away from the things that did matter. What's that they say about being a work in progress?

Luke had a PE class first period, so he was probably down at the gym already. I walked up the main corridor to my first period class, Speech and Communications. Most of my theatre kids were in that class, but there were also a few future lawyers and politicians. That's how I described the students from a more privileged background who understood the power of words and how important it was to learn how to harness that power.

I walked in and calmed the kids down and asked them to take their seats. We usually started Mondays with a little round table discussion of current events from the previous week, so I perched on the corner of my desk and asked "All right, who's got something for us?"

"I do," said Jett Winthrop, hand raised. "It's a 'Blind Gossip' item."

The other students giggled. Jett tended to stick to pop culture and sports figures in his news items, while the future lawyers always brought up political events and business news. The theatre kids hovered between the two, trying to appease both the high and lowbrow crowds.

"All right," I said. "Well, I'm not sure gossip is something we want to concentrate on in this class. Anyone have anything of more substance?"

"Oh, I think you'll like this one," he smirked. He was staring me down, and I flinched. I could feel it. Shit. Why did I take this job? Oh, yes, it was either this or prison guard. But what's the difference, actually?

"What is it?" one of the girls asked. "More Tom Cruise stuff? Justin Bieber?"

"No, this one's local," he said. He was enjoying this. Before I could think of what to do, he began reciting, as if he ran his own celebrity gossip blog. "These two confirmed bachelors were recently spotted eating out together on the town. By the looks they were shooting across the table, anyone could assume they're shooting their love guns in the Greek style back at their shared abode, that is when they aren't out sharing a love run by the lake. Guess who, don't sue!"

The class erupted. They started calling out names. Local politicians, celebrities, newscasters, the weatherman, sports figures. Everything except teachers. We were standing right in front of them, and right now I was so grateful that they didn't even think we had private lives. I was just the warden for this particular hour, and then they forgot about me. But Jett didn't forget anything. He saw me and Luke arriving together, he saw us running together, and now his mother saw us eating out at the Tater Tot, and she had obviously shared that with her son, or talked about it within earshot.

The room fell into chaos with discussions over the subject of forced outings and whether it was the correct thing to do in a modern society or if we should just ignore the obvious. I had lost control. I heard nothing, and everything. I was too shocked to react as Jett just sat there, staring me down with a wicked grin, as I looked back at him, frozen.

"Mr. Walter? *Mr. Walter!*" The voice came from the door. "Mr. Walter, is there a problem here? We've had some complaints about noise."

I turned. Snapped out of it. Bammy was standing at my door. The kids had quieted down, and Jett's wicked grin had been replaced with the false face of an innocent angel.

"No, Miss Talbot," I said, quickly snapping back to the present. "No problems. Just a little moment of levity that got out of hand." I stood from my desk and turned back to my students. "Let's get back to work now, class. Please pull out your essays on the current state of US/Soviet relations. Jett? You're up first. Let's go."

■ ■ ■

When I got back to Luke's that night, I found him already sitting on the couch with a beer in his hand, legs propped up on the coffee table. He had opened a bottle of red wine and placed a full glass out, waiting for me.

"Hey, babe," I said, as I threw myself down beside him. "Shit day?"

"Two words," he said. "Chip Carter."

"Jett Winthrop," I countered. He clinked his beer bottle to my wine glass and we both took big sips. Then another.

"You go first," he said.

I told him about Jett's "Blind Gossip" item, and that he must have overheard something Amber said. It was obvious he was trying to shake me, and sadly, it worked.

"Shit," said Luke, and took another swig from his bottle. "Mine wasn't much better. Chip is on my track team. We had a practice last period, and we always meet in the locker room after to confirm time results, hear pointers, talk strategies, you name it. Well, during my wrap up, Chip decided to strip down to his jock and stand there with one leg propped up on a bench, showing the world his prized package. When I asked him to cover up with a towel for modesty he said, 'What's the matter, Coach? We're all men here. Unless someone here *likes* men.' He stared straight at me. The team started snickering and I had to shut them up with threats of extra laps. Horseplay is fine when we're not working, but this was a meeting and I told them I expected them to pay attention. I couldn't get out of there fast enough."

"We're screwed, aren't we?" I asked, feeling defeated.

"No, Derek. We're not," he said, his anger growing. "They've got another thing coming if they think I'm going to back down this easily. Yeah, they surprised us with a one two punch. But now we know they're coming for us. They're amateurs, and I'm a professional. I'm getting another beer, and then we're talking formations."

"Put me in, Coach. I'm ready to play." And I topped off my glass.

■ ■ ■

"Are you sure you want to do this?" I asked, as we pulled into the high school parking lot. I had left Willie at Luke's place, and we came to school together in his Jeep.

"Does a bear like honey?" he answered.

"Well, yeah, but what you're planning isn't going to get us any honey, babe," I said. "Just expect an onslaught of bees. Or hornets. Wasps, even. Like, millions of wasps all up in our business, stinging the shit out of us when they don't get their way."

"I can handle some insects, Derek. I've got big 'ole hands to swat 'em away. Besides, you're worth it. This is what I want. I promise."

Shit. Here goes. I opened the car door and stepped out. It was a warm early spring day, and the sun was shining in full force, with just a slight cool breeze. The parking lot was full of students gathering their things, catching up with friends and making their way slowly to the school doors.

"We who are about to die, salute you," I mumbled.

"What's that?"

"Nothing."

We were standing at the front of the car, and he reached down and grasped my hand. Damn. The moment he did that, it just made all the crazy stuff in the world go away. I turned to look at his beautiful blue eyes, and I suddenly knew he was right. Here I was, trying to hold him back, when all he wanted was *out*. Had I forgotten how that felt? Had I forgotten that crazy euphoric rush of just being able to be who you really are, express how you feel, *love* someone without fear?

I remembered the first time I went to a gay dance club in New York City. I had lied to my best friend, Reggie, and told him I was busy and had plans with work colleagues. I remember looking at the club from across the street, casing it, checking out the types of people who went in and out. I was petrified, and it must have taken me twenty-five minutes to get up the courage to cross that street. I remember thinking that the doorman would judge me. He would 'know.' Truthfully? All he wanted to do was check my ID and send me to the next line so they could take my money. When I crossed that threshold, I did not burst into flames, my world did not end, and my self-loathing began to subside, just a little. I hid in the shadows and nursed a vodka and soda, but when an Erasure song came on, all bets were off. The lights bounced off the disco ball, I found my little corner of the dance floor, and a whole new world opened up. I never looked back.

We walked from the parking lot towards the front entrance, holding hands. My heart was beating a mile a minute. I could only imagine that his was about to jump out of his chest. There were no screams from the students, no foul cries. It was as if they didn't even notice, actually. We paused at the door, and he turned to me.

"Have a great day, babe," he said. "See you tonight."

And he kissed me. Not a rock star sending me off at the airport kind of kiss, but not a quiet, chaste peck on the cheek, either. It was a kiss. A real kiss. A lover's kiss. A kiss that said *I love this man. He's mine. And I don't give a shit who doesn't like that.*

He released me, turned in the opposite direction and marched towards the gym, while I lingered there a moment too long. Weak in the knees, I composed myself and headed towards my first period class. As I did, I walked right past Jett and Chip, the best of friends. They witnessed the whole thing.

It took about ten minutes, we estimated later, before the whole school knew.

We had agreed, together, to only say one thing when confronted.

"Yes, I'm in a relationship with Mr. Walter/Coach Walcott. However, our private lives are off limits. We are here to teach/coach. No more questions. Let's get back to work."

■ ■ ■

"Derek, Luke, I guess you both know why I called you here today. Why didn't you tell me you were going to pull this stunt beforehand?"

It was the end of the day, and Luke and I had both received urgent messages to meet in Bammy's office after school. It wasn't a surprise, but still, it didn't bode well for us.

"Because we knew you'd try and stop us," I offered, in way of an excuse. "I like your new office, by the way. Bigger than the last one. Are you keeping those curtains, though?"

"Derek, stop it! I'm trying to be serious, here," she said, arms crossed over her chest, covering the monogram on her sweater. "This is a serious discussion." Her face conveyed that she was telling the truth. This whole conversation pained her.

I composed myself and looked her squarely in the face. Luke was sitting next to me with his back so rigid you would think he was meeting the president. He just stared ahead with military precision, jaw tight, temples throbbing to the beat of his heart.

"Now, all these kids have cell phones," she started. "You know that. They spent most of the day texting each other everything they could piece together. Your fellow teachers aren't pleased. The whole day was a wash. You two are the topic on everyone's lips."

"It's nice to be loved?" I said, but she was over my humor.

"Derek, the parents have started calling." Bammy looked unhappy. Her voice was rigid. Cold. She didn't like one moment of this. I could see it in her eyes. She was trying hard to balance friendship and work, but the work was going to win. I could feel it. "They've called an emergency school board meeting tonight. Thankfully it's a closed session, but it's only a few weeks before we have another open session, and you can bet we're expecting fireworks at that one."

She softened her tone. "You know I love you two. I do. But I have these responsibilities. Especially since Bellman has left me this job, temporarily. It's not really mine until he's elected mayor. And I know that's going to happen, it's just… Derek, I *need* this job. I love it. I can do good things here. I know I can. But y'all have to help me out a little. What were you thinking?!" She buried her face in her hands, exasperated.

"It was me, Bammy." Luke spoke up. I turned to look at him. "My sister, Lana, threatened to out us. She and Amber. It was her way of trying to shut me up. But I can't do that. Not anymore. I was too quiet my whole life. I'm not trying to 'corrupt the youth' or cause any scandal, and I certainly don't have any agenda to push. But I'm happy, Bammy. I'm in love. With this man, sitting here. Your friend. And if my colleagues can bring their spouses to work, and meet them out for drinks, and have dinner with them in public places, then I deserve those same rights. I'm just standing up, Bammy. That's all. Just standing up."

It sounded so simple when he said it. Just standing up. Being counted. He mattered. *We* mattered. And he was tired of hiding, putting all of that energy into creative little white lies and stories. It was exhausting, and I knew it.

"Y'all are gonna kill me," she said, finally, giving up. "I love you both. I do. But this is gonna be the death of me. All right. Let's put our brains together and figure out what to do. Drinks, tomorrow? I'll fill you in on this school board meeting. But no more make out sessions in the halls. Just for now, okay? Until we have a plan. Please?"

We stood up and gathered our jackets. I gave her a warm hug that we held for just a few seconds longer than necessary. We separated, but she continued to hold me by the shoulders and she looked up at me with a very serious face.

"But, seriously. If I *was* gonna change these curtains, what would you suggest?"

■ ■ ■

They called themselves the CCCP. The "Committee of Concerned Caring Parents." Though the school board session was closed, word spread fast. Southern ladies can organize a bake sale in a few hours on any given day, so amassing a troop to combat the spread of salacious homosexual liberal influence over their precious unsullied offspring was certainly not too difficult. It's a bit like the old fire brigade systems in small towns. The leader gets the first call, he or she calls two more people, those caring citizens call two more each, and before you know it, you have the whole town informed. Mobs rule in the South, and this mob had plenty of moms. There's a reason Tennessee is called the Volunteer State. Unfortunately for us, this particular group was spearheaded by two very strong women who knew Luke very well. Lana Walcott and Amber Winthrop were following through on their threats, big time.

It's no surprise that the CCCP was hastily formed to represent that comfortable old Southern notion of "family values," and to protect the "traditional family role" and lament the "loss of morality" in our present day society. Franklin Graham would be so proud. The funny thing was, Lana was single with no children, and not only had Amber been divorced three times, but she had "dated" most of the eligible men in town, at least twice. The level of hypocrisy was enormous, but unspoken. All that mattered was surface appearance, and they had plenty of angry citizens ready to stand up for the "moral standards" which they preached, but obviously did not practice. My hands were sore from all the finger quotes.

Luke and I knew we were courting trouble, but no amount of mental awareness can prepare you for the reality of a huge crowd shouting vile things at you as you step from your car at your place of work. The Parkville Police had been called in to make sure that the students and teachers could enter and exit the school safely, but they really weren't prepared for what they encountered. The CCCP had really rallied the troops. They were the only ones there. There was no opposition, no counter message, no support for love or equality or basic civil rights. Just chaos and signs and yelling and reporters. Plenty of reporters. Did we underestimate the chaos we had brought?

It was a struggle to make it to the door, cameras and microphones shoved in our faces the entire way. Luke had his arm around me the whole time, protecting me. Bammy was standing just inside the school, waiting for us.

"Well. Good morning," she said, tight lipped, arms crossed. "Are you boys happy?" I looked at her, shell shocked. No, Bammy. I'm not happy at all. In fact, I'm officially pissed off.

7

LOW TEA

Bammy ushered us into her office, quickly, and for once, Miss Mabel actually looked up as we passed by, removing her reading glasses and letting them swing by the silver chain on her neck.

"Listen," I started, when she had closed the door behind us, "before you start yelling at us, may I remind you what year this is?"

"Derek, just stop," said Bammy, sternly. "Let me speak before you tear into me, all right? I'm on your side. Just give me a break, okay? It was a pretty crappy night and my day isn't looking any brighter."

Luke held my hand tighter and gave me a look that told me to calm down. Yelling at Bammy wasn't going to help. I knew that. But my killer instincts were taking over, and I wasn't interested in remaining silent. My man and I had been threatened, and I was ready for a fight.

I grew up in this town. This was my home, my school. These are my friends. I've known these people for years.

But suddenly I was the enemy? Suddenly Luke and I were the very thing that was going to bring down modern civilization, as we know it? It was absurd. After having spent so many years up North, I had truly forgotten the lengths at which people could express their ignorance and hatred. Well, this was certainly an unwelcome reminder.

"I went to the school board meeting last night as acting principal of Parkville High," she said, "but I want you to know that I was also there as your friend and your supporter. It's a game, Derek. It's politics. It sucks. I know it. But I had to put on one face and try to play the game in our favor, with my true face hidden and without giving too much away. It wasn't easy. Some of those board members were out for blood. People who you and I know damn well are some of the biggest hypocrites in town. Liars, cheats, adulterers, you name it. Heck, I wouldn't be surprised if one or two of them are secretly gay. But that's the key word, guys. 'Secretly.' You broke that unwritten rule. You know you did. Now we need to figure our way out of this mess."

I was taken aback. I didn't expect this outrage, that our one simple kiss could create such a storm. I don't think that Luke did, either. He was stoic, but I could sense that he was shaken. He had been admired his whole life. Looked up to. Adored. He was the football hero of Parkville High. This was all new to him, but I also knew that there was no way he was stepping back. When he stepped up to a challenge, Luke was all in.

"So what's the deal, Bammy?" he asked. "Are you firing us?"

She paused as she searched for the words. She took a deep breath and said, "No. Your jobs are safe. For now.

But there are a few rules we need to put into place if we're gonna get through this."

"Rules?" I asked. "Like what?"

"First," she said, "no PDA. No public displays of affection. Nada. That includes handholding. You understand? Now, before you start in on me again, I know that's not fair. Yes, other straight couples kiss. Even the students hold hands. I know that. But these people aren't ready to listen to a sane argument right now, okay? Second? And this one just pains me to even say the words. They are calling it 'Don't Say Gay.' There's to be no discussion, no mention, not even an allusion to homosexuality at all on school property. None. We don't discuss it, at all. If it comes up, change the subject and tell the students they need to get that information from their parents or their church. And finally, the third rule. Any student who wishes to withdraw from one of your classes or sports teams may do so at any time this semester, with absolutely zero consequences to their academic record."

She stopped talking. I was stunned. We both were. These "rules" were ridiculous.

"Derek? Luke? I'm so sorry. I really am." She was sincere in her apology, but not going to bend. I could see that. "This was the best I could do under pressure. Believe me. I tried my hardest. Unfortunately, I've been given the task to present these guidelines to you today, and if they are not acceptable, well, honestly, I don't want to even talk about that part." She paused. Silence. "Guys? Waddya say? Can we adhere to these until the end of this semester? The school board would like your confirmation of these rules today, in writing, and then we will revisit them before school starts again in the fall."

Luke turned to look at me. It was as if I could read his mind, and he knew it. He loved his job. Coaching meant everything to him. I squeezed his hand, and just nodded, once.

"We'll sign it, Bammy," he said, turning back to face her, his jaw still tight. "But I want you to know something. There is no way we're accepting this quietly. We are going to fight this in every possible legal way we can, and some underhanded ways, as well."

"I hope you *do* fight this," she said, narrowing her eyes. "I really hope you do. And I will be the first to cheer you on when you win."

■ ■ ■

The rest of the day was as awful as you could imagine. I went straight to my Speech and Communications class, and the first topic the students tried to discuss was the protesters. There were arguments for and against, of course, but I had to stop the discussion before they went any further. Jett was sitting back in his seat, arms behind his head, grinning as if he was on top of the world. One day, kid, you'll get yours. Trust me.

I skipped the lunchroom. I didn't feel like facing my fellow teachers at our communal table, so I ate my sandwich in an empty classroom. Bammy had me so paranoid and freaked out that I was afraid to even find Luke to make sure he was okay. I was worried about him. I was used to putting up with years of absurd hatred from misguided idiots, but this was all new to him. He puts on a brave, strong face, but that man is a sweetheart on the inside, and I was really angry that he had to go through this.

My Advanced Acting class was the one period I was looking forward to. I had a surprise for them, and I wasn't sure how they would take it.

"Hi, kids," I started as I entered the room. "Settle down. Seats please. I know there's been a lot of excitement today, but we have lots to do."

"Mr. Walter?" One of the boys spoke up. "This is just BS. We want you to know that. We all think this is just stupid." There was a round of applause and agreements all around.

I put my hand over my face. Shit. This was hard. When Luke and I made the decision to stand up for who we are we didn't really take into account the lives that would be affected, outside our respective families. Well, in a way, these kids are my family, too. I was naive to forget that.

"Thank you," I responded, quietly. "There's a lot I'd like to say, of course, but you should know I've been restricted in that area. It means a lot to me, your support. It does. So I hope you won't be upset with me with some news I need to share now."

The room was silent. I had their full attention.

"As you know, the spring play is coming up. I already announced that we are putting on *Death of a Salesman*, and many of you have been practicing your monologues for the auditions at the end of this week. But I'm sorry to say I've had a change of heart. *Death* is out. We're doing *The Crucible*, instead."

Changing plans like that had to hurt. I had basically cast the parts for *Death of a Salesman* in my head, and many of the students already understood what parts they were right for. Some had even begun memorizing lines. But this threw a wrench into their plans. I stood there, unsure of their reactions.

A hand rose from their seats. "That's the play about the witch hunt, right?" one of my senior girls asked.

"Yes, it is."

"Way to go, Mr. Walter." A slow burn smile spread across her face. "We'll show them!"

Indeed, we will.

■ ■ ■

Luke and I met up after school to support each other every night that week. The toll of putting on a brave face during the day was catching up with both of us. He was too stubborn to reach out to Lana and Amber, but I had to agree with him, for now. Everything was too fresh at the moment, and both sides just needed some time to calm down. The protests at school began to subside, although there was still a small but strong showing from the CCCP each morning as we arrived at school, separately. We drove our own cars, now, and barely spoke on campus. Some of our fellow teachers treated us differently, with a palpable lack of respect. I had known Mrs. Powell, the music teacher, since I was fourteen years old. Now, she would barely look at me. It would be hard to explain to an outsider. They still liked us, however we had broken that rule of golden silence. Everything would have been fine if we had just kept it all hidden, as it "should be."

I was still spending a few nights a week in my old bedroom at Mom's place. I pulled the car into my parking spot in the driveway and walked around to the side door entrance, off the porch. Mom was sitting outside reading the *Parkville Post*, a glass of sweet tea by her side. I plopped down in the chair next to her and she folded her paper and put it down.

"Well, honey," she said wearily, "I always said that you knew how to make an entrance. All eyes are on you now, huh? How's it feel?"

"Just great, Mom. As I'm sure you can imagine."

She reached out and put her hand on my knee. "Just be strong, sweetie. I know you can find your way through this. Heck, if you can handle New York City, I'm sure you can handle Parkville."

"I'm not so sure of that," I said, dejectedly. "I'm kind of outnumbered here. And Parkville doesn't play fair."

"No, they don't," she said. "There's an article in the paper today about Eddie Bellman's candidacy for mayor. He's focusing on 'family values,' of course. Says he wants to go ahead with Mayor Tazewell's rezoning plans to clean up the city."

"This whole town is crazy. Truly. You have no idea."

"Well, I know someone who has your back," she said. "And I'm pretty sure he can give you some guidance. Why don't you go talk to your uncle tonight? He's at his club."

This was new territory for me, and I pulled back and gave her a face. Of course my mom knew her brother was gay. She had to. But we had never discussed it, of course.

"How much exactly do you know about Barry?" I asked, unsure of how much I should say.

"Oh, sweetie. The two of you, honestly. You both think I just walk around sleepwalking all the time, which I admit isn't super far off, but I do have eyes. My brother has more jewelry on his dressing table than I do. Heck, I've even borrowed some. And Janey's feet were not that big."

I laughed. She was right. I needed some guidance, and hopefully Beret was the right woman for the job.

"But let's get you fed before you head on out," she said. "Regardless of what my brother thinks, vodka isn't a meal, even if you do pair it with tomato juice, a stalk of celery and a handful of olives. How about some pork chops and fried okra?"

"Oh, Mom, you can make food sound like poetry, you know that?"

She giggled, and we stood up together and walked into the house, her hand in mine.

■ ■ ■

With a belly happily full of Southern love, I drove Willie to the Bears' Club and parked out back. I didn't even bother trying to come in through the front, anymore, now that I knew about the red lacquered door that led backstage.

Beret was onstage singing *Cabaret*. She was actually singing this time, and not lip-syncing. Her deep voice worked really well for the song. She was dressed in a sparkly black pantsuit, very Liza Minelli, with a short, black, cropped pixie wig. I half expected Belle to follow through on the 1970's theme and trot out on stage after her dressed as Bianca Jagger on a white horse, but then I remembered she reportedly made that famous entrance semi nude, and the mental image of Bellman naked shuddered me back to reality.

The crowd watching the show applauded, and Beret announced that it was time for a little cocktail break. She spotted me out of the corner of her smoky eye and then encouraged everyone to go to the bar for some liquid sanity.

"Well hello, Dolly!" she gushed, grabbing me in her arms as she exited stage right. "What brings you to my neck of the woods tonight?"

"I was hoping for a little of that liquid sanity, you just mentioned," I said. "And maybe some advice?"

"You got it, kid. Scotty?" Taking charge, as usual, she motioned for her trusty stage manager, never far from earshot. "*Do* be a doll and bring around some cocktails for us, will you? I'm feeling feisty tonight. WWLD?!"

"WWLD?" he asked.

"*What Would Liza Do*, darling! Vodka, of course. Is there anything else? Just tell the bartender. He'll set us up. My nephew and I will be downstairs in my dressing room." And off we went, down the rabbit hole.

Scotty followed soon after with a tray of drinks and lemon drop shooters, and we started right in.

"So, Dolly. Cheers!" We clinked our glasses.

"Now tell me," she asked, getting right to the point, "what the *hell* were you thinking?"

"Thanks, Uncle Barry. Just dive right in. No need to sugar coat it, huh?"

"Well, kid, you really stepped in it this time." She took a long sip and smirked at me. "I mean, it's one thing to be gay, it's another thing to be out and gay. But you've gone a step further than most people in this town. You've 'flaunted' it, proudly, and that just ain't Southern. They can't just overlook that." She could see the look in my eyes. This wasn't the advice I expected. "Now don't get mad at me. You *know* I love you, but there are certain ways of doing things down here that you may have forgotten from your time in the big city."

"I know, I know," I said, "but this is ludicrous. 'Family values?' Who are they kidding?"

"Well, themselves, of course. That's who," she said, matter-of-factly. "And their neighbors, their kids, their pastors, their friends. All of them. But that's part of the game. That's how we play it down here. Look at Eddie Bellman, for example. He's running for mayor as a conservative, which of course he is. But that's just one facet. One façade, shall we say? Here, in this world, he's Belle, and even though he's a cross dresser and a stage hog, we all respect his choices, because he doesn't 'flaunt' them out in the real world. Oh, I wish it wasn't this way. I truly do. I don't know how to change it. I don't know how to fix it. I'd say you are doing the right thing, though. It will only take another generation before all of this is just trifle. Nonsense. No one will care, anymore. But someone has to step up and be the trendsetter, and you, my darling nephew, seem to have taken on that role in Parkville. And I'm *proud* of you. I really am."

"Thanks, Beret. A lot of good that does, though."

"Now tell me, how are you holding up?" she asked. "And Luke? That poor boy probably doesn't know what hit him."

"I'm fine. I've been through this garbage before. But it's all new to Luke. He's strong. I have no doubts about that. But he's not used to being on the losing team."

"Well, he takes after his father on that one. Red Walcott never did like losing." She took another long sip and set her glass down. "Did I ever tell you how Red and I met?"

"Not really," I answered. "You just said that you and Janey were friends with Red and Posy for years. But not much else."

"We were all in high school together, of course. Red was the big man on campus. Star athlete. I played football, too, but not as well as Red. I had a hell of a kicking leg. Still do!" With that, she extended her black pantsuit clad leg high in the air. "We grew up in this town, so we had known each other, of course, but we were never really close. Eventually, he and Posy and Janey and I began double dating, and we all became good friends. Very good friends. The 1970s were very political, you know. Wars, race relations, lots of inequality. We both had an interest in politics. Red saw it as a possible career, I saw it as a way to affect some positive change. Maybe you get that from me? Anyway, he and I put our heads together and formed the Little Dicks, to support Richard Nixon."

"Wait. 'The Little Dicks?' You're kidding me, right?"

"Beautiful, isn't it? It was my idea, of course. Stroke of genius, if I do say so myself. See, Dolly, we just have to be a bit more intelligent than our enemies. That's the difference between 'flaunting' and expressing your real intentions, without actually saying them."

"I think I'm beginning to understand."

"Good." She finished her cocktail, the remaining ice cubes spinning in her glass. "Nixon was a disaster, of course. Red was angry. He hated being wrong. But he is a man who learns, and you saw that when Luke came out to him. Red came around. He's conservative, but he's also definitely compassionate. I'm sure Posy would have felt the same, and Lana will see the light eventually, too."

"I need to get Luke and his sister together," I said. "We have to solve this thing."

"That's a good idea, Dolly. Just don't forget the liquid refreshments," she said. "Those Walcotts can lean pretty far to the right, and you'll need her a little loosened up if you're going to make any headway. Another round?"

"I thought you'd never ask."

8

LANA BANANA

School continued to be as fun-free as you can imagine.

Jett took every opportunity he could to disrupt my class, and Chip was still being an absolute douche around Luke, but both of us had our hands tied by these stupid rules we had agreed to follow. The kids could drop out of our classes or teams at any time with no repercussions, so why should they behave? It was sanctioned anarchy.

My Advanced Acting class was enjoying working on *The Crucible*. They were smart enough to see the parallels between the witch hunt in the play, the McCarthy Communist hearings of the 1950s and the current situation that Luke and I were facing, without me having to say a word. I was really proud of them, again.

After my talk with Beret, I knew I had to try and get Luke and Lana together, so I pushed him to call her and set something up. He was stubborn, but he agreed that someone needed to take the first step. Yes, we had to stand up for our rights, but family is important, and he needed to try and make some headway with her.

He gave her a call after school one day, and surprisingly, she answered the phone. She even agreed to let him come over and talk again.

"What are you going to say?" I asked.

"I just need to reason with her. We're family."

"Barry suggested a few drinks. Bring a bottle or two with you."

"Good idea," he said. "We can stop at the liquor store on the way."

"Wait. We?" I asked. "You're not planning on bringing me, are you?"

"Why not? I need your support, babe. And I want her to get to know you. If we weren't dating, I wouldn't be in this situation. I needed to come out publicly. You understand that, but she doesn't, yet. Our relationship is my whole reason for fighting this ridiculous protest, anyway, and I think if she gets to know you like I have, she'll understand that."

"Luke, I don't think that's the best idea. You can't force me on her. If she's ever going to accept this, it has to be her idea."

"Well, let's hope a few drinks soften her up, then. Come on. Grab your coat and put on your best Southern charm."

Great. Southern charm, I can do. I just hope I don't end up as another silver souvenir dangling from her bracelet.

■ ■ ■

Lana lived out west near her father in a condo that butted right up to the golf course at the Parkville Country Club. An interior designer by trade, she used the club as a sort of office-at-large, since most of her clients were members, anyway. When she wasn't on site supervising the transformation of a house or office, she was easy to find by the pool, in the restaurant, or at the bar, and always dressed appropriately. Whereas Sun Tzu practiced *The Art of War*, Lana practiced tennis and yoga, and she used those skills to attract new clients.

Luke pulled the car into a visitor's spot, and we stepped out. He didn't appear visibly nervous, but I sure was. I was skittish enough around his sister in high school. As a teenager I was so quiet and shy that anyone who was considered popular terrified me, regardless of his or her age. Now that I was the gay guy who used his wicked ways to mesmerize her brother into switching teams, I was even more apprehensive about this meeting.

The doorbell rang, and it was one of those custom chimes that make you say to yourself *Oh, God, really*? The chime had a familiar singsong to it, but it wasn't familiar enough to have a title that you could associate with it. It was just an earworm that wouldn't go away and it was competing with the sound of my heart beating out of my chest. Luke squeezed my hand, but I felt like I couldn't move. The door swung open.

"Hey, Lana Banana," he said, trying to set the tone.

"What's *he* doing here?" She wasn't smiling. Well hello to you, too.

Luke sighed, undeterred. "Lana, I invited Derek. May we come in?"

In lieu of a response, she simply stepped to the side and waved us in, without a word. She stuck her head out the door and did a quick left right. Heaven forbid anyone see us? It was going to take a miracle to bring these two back together.

"We brought some vodka, Cointreau and cranberry," Luke said, offering the goods we picked up from the liquor store.

"I used to work in a bar in college," I offered, trying to make some headway. "I can make a pretty mean Cosmo."

"What, no little paper umbrellas?" She said sarcastically as she turned on her heels and walked towards the kitchen. Luke turned back to me and made a face. At least she was attempting humor. Maybe there was some hope, after all?

He placed the bag down on the island in the kitchen and I scooted around to the other side, leaving them standing together. She was staring at him with her arms folded across her chest and a scowl on her face. He had his hands in his jean pockets and a shy grin on his face, and I wondered if those dimples and blue eyes affected her in the same way they did me?

He reached his arms out to hug her and she playfully batted him away.

"No," she said, petulantly. "I'm so *pissed* at you. How could you *do* this to me?"

"Lana, I didn't *do anything* to you. I did something for me. What choice did you give me? You basically threatened me with a life of silence, and I wasn't going to have that anymore. I'd done that for too many years. I needed to come clean."

She looked angry. "Don't you see that you've embarrassed yourself, Luke? Embarrassed the family? How could you?"

Appearances were everything to Lana Walcott. In high school she always had the right purse, the right clothes, the right friends following at just the right number of steps behind. Everything she ever wanted was handed to her, but now she was facing something she didn't want, and her big brother was going to suffer for it, not her.

She turned away from him and walked over to the white satin sofa and positioned herself regally, one arm stretched across the back, knees together, her legs crossed at the ankles. Luke followed and sat on the second couch, opposite. It was a Walcott Face Off. Who would budge first? I busied myself with making drinks, just wishing I could disappear.

"I don't know what you expect to accomplish here," she said. "What is this? A slumber party? Is a pizza delivery boy going to show up and strip for us? Are we going to paint each others' nails?"

She was digging in, being nasty to see if she could get a rise out of him. Outwardly she was acting like she was enjoying it, but it didn't seem genuine. Hurting him wouldn't help her feel better, and he could see that. She was a wounded animal, just lashing out.

"If that's what you want, sure," he said, calmly, not taking the bait. "It's not my thing, but if it will make you feel better, I'd try anything for you, Lana. You know that."

"What happened to you, big brother?"

"Nothing, Lana," he answered. "I'm still the same Luke. I'm just more honest now about who I am and what I want."

I placed a tray of Cosmopolitans down on the coffee table between the sofas, but neither of them moved. Lana was staring intently at Luke, unflinching in her steely resolve.

"Is this the part where we say what *Sex and the City* character we are?" she asked, pointedly. "*I'm* Carrie." She was really taking this as far as she could.

"Maybe I should step out for a bit," I offered. "Give you two some room."

"That'd be great," she said coldly, without even looking at me. "This is a family matter. Back entrance is that way." She flung her left hand up and pointed behind her.

"Derek, please sit down with me. I'd like you here." Luke looked up at me and gave me a pleading look. I was uncomfortable, but this was for him. For us. He wanted us to try and fix it, together.

I sat down next to him on the couch and he leaned forward, interlacing his fingers and placing his forearms on his knees, really looking her in the eyes, again.

"Lana, I know what you're doing, and it won't work. You did this to me when we were kids, and it didn't work then, either. You can poke and prod and bug me all you want, but I won't break. Remember those staring contests we had? I won every time. You'd get distracted or bored or thirsty and just walk off. We'd sit in the back of the car on trips and you'd poke me, non-stop from home to church, during the service and then back again, but I never cared. I gave up even locking my bedroom door, because you'd jimmy it open or start knocking non-stop or just walk in whenever you'd please. I let you get away with everything, Lana. Maybe I shouldn't have, but I loved you. I still do.

You're my little sister, and I'll do anything to protect you and make sure you're happy, even at my own expense. But maybe things need to change, now. I can't protect you anymore, like I did when we were kids. I'm trying to be honest with you here. I'm not asking you to embrace this with open arms, just yet. It's still taking Father and Rosa some time. But you can at least try and meet me halfway. Can you do that for me?"

She relaxed her body language, just a touch. Something he said had found its way inside of her, and she appeared to be mulling it over.

"I can't believe you told Daddy and Rosa before me," she admitted, softly. "That hurt, Luke. That *hurt* me. I'm your sister. We share everything."

"I'm sorry, Lana. I didn't plan it that way on purpose. I wasn't thinking clearly at the time. A lot happened really fast with Derek, and I was trying to fix a situation that I didn't think was fixable. I should have spoken to you all at once. I am sorry about that. Really, I am."

We seemed to have reached an impasse. She remained quiet, thinking. Her face still held a steady scowl, but she no longer looked like she was going to pounce. I just wish she had taken a few sips of that drink. I know how badly I wanted mine right now, but I wasn't going to be the only one reaching for the booze.

"You were supposed to marry Amber, Luke."

"Seriously? You gotta be kidding me, now." He shook his head. "Amber? Did you forget that she cheated on me in college, and the product of that pairing just happens to be Jett, who's currently terrorizing Derek? Honestly. I can't believe you'd wish Amber on anyone." He leaned back and placed his hands on his knees, clearly frustrated. She didn't respond and the silence grew unbearable between them, again. I wanted so badly to reach for that drink, but I didn't dare. Finally, he spoke up. "Excuse me. I'm a bit... I need to go use the bathroom. Will you two be all right?"

"Yeah, of course," I said, lying. Lana said nothing.

He kissed me on the cheek as he rose to leave, and I could see the look of horror on her face. For every step forward we had just taken, we were about to take two steps back.

A good ninety seconds of uncomfortable silence passed before she looked at me squarely in the eyes and said, "I blame you."

"Really? I blame Tarzan," I said, finally finding my voice. I reached down for that Cosmo and took a healthy sip.

"What?" she snapped.

"Nothing. You wouldn't understand."

"Oh, I understand enough." Here it comes. "I know your type. You saw a handsome rich guy and you did everything you could to snare him. You saw a big payday. You *confused* him, messed with his mind. I've seen it before. And now he wants me to 'get to know' you? But you know what? You mean nothing to me. Nothing. The only person who matters to me is my brother. This isn't about being straight or gay or bi. I could care less who he sleeps with. This is about my brother and my family. *You* don't matter to me. At all. You're insignificant. And no matter how hard you try, you will never, *ever* be good enough for him. And I will do everything in my power to make sure he sees the light."

"LANA! That's about enough." Luke was standing at the hall, just steps from us. There was no telling how long he had been standing there listening to her diatribe. I was in shock. This wasn't about being gay, at all? Is that what she said? She just thinks I'm a gold digger?

"*Derek, let's go.*" Luke's voice rang out in the room. "I think we've overstayed our welcome. I don't want to hang around where my boyfriend isn't welcome."

We walked out without saying another word, and he slammed the door forcefully behind us.

Luke unlocked the car remotely with his keychain and walked over to the passenger seat and opened the door for me. Always the gentleman, even when he was stressed. He closed my door and walked around and climbed into the driver's seat, but his hands just gripped the wheel while he stared ahead, not moving.

"I'm sorry about that," he said. "That stuff she was spouting at the end. I don't believe it. She doesn't know you like I do. She's just worried about getting her hands on Father's money, but it's more than that. When Mother died, she felt abandoned. They sent us to therapy. Rosa filled the space, but things were never exactly the same. Does she think that I am abandoning her now? Is that it? Because this is obviously about me and not you. I'm so sorry, babe."

"It's okay," I said, quietly. "I didn't expect that either."

He started the car, but still didn't put it into gear. I could see the wheels spinning in his head.

"Luke?"

"Yeah," he answered, with more than a hint of anger still in his voice.

"Are you open to just one nugget of advice?" I asked.

"Not really," he answered.

"Well, you're getting it. In the future, when someone asks you what *Sex and the City* character you are, the instinct is always to say Carrie, because she was the star of the show. But really, it's Miranda. She got everything she wanted in the end. A house, a loving husband, a kid, a nanny, a car, a great career. What did Carrie get? A handsome man who left her at the altar and a lot of shoes. I'd take Miranda's deal, any day."

He turned to look at me.

"You're really messed up. And I love you," he said. "You know that?"

"Yeah. I do."

He put the car in gear and we started towards home.

■ ■ ■

"We can put on a show!" Kit exclaimed.

"Hold up, y'all," I said. "This isn't a Judy Garland/ Mickey Rooney musical from the 1940s."

We were gathered in our regular booth at the Firelight. Me, Luke, Tommy, Meredith, Kit and Shawn. Bammy and Michael were out on their own, but honestly, it just felt like she was laying low for a bit, on purpose. I understood, all too well.

"No, silly!" Kit placed her beer down, for emphasis. "A fundraiser! At the gallery! Meredith and I want to donate the space so you can raise money for your lawsuit, if you need to go forward with that, ya know?"

Luke jumped into the conversation. "That's sweet of you, but we don't need any money. We've got that part covered. I've had a few conversations with my father's lawyer, but he suggests we wait a bit to see how this plays out, rather than cause more friction by making the first move. I'm inclined to agree."

"Okay," said Meredith, slowly. "So you don't need money. That's cool. So instead of raising cash, let's raise awareness!" Her hands were flailing about, excitedly. "Let's put together a super cool night with strippers and drag queens and artists and really show Parkville how much support you two have in the community."

I turned to Luke to gauge his reaction.

"How 'bout it, babe?" I squeezed his knee under the table. He reached for my hand and held it in his.

"Let's do it," he said, defiantly.

And the Love All benefit was born.

9

LOVE ALL

It was the night of the big event, and I was a little nervous.

Since most of my stuff was still at Mom's place, I went there to get ready for the evening. It was so important for me to have her and Uncle Barry by my side, and they both wanted to come and support Luke and me.

"What should I wear?" my mom asked, as she rifled through her closets. I was sitting on her bed, just an hour before I was supposed to go over to Luke's.

"Do you have anything sparkly?" I suggested. "It's kind of an arty night. Not too crazy, but not too conservative, either. I mean, there won't be anyone in tuxedos and ball gowns."

"I hope not," she said with a grimace. "I can't compete with that crap. You know that. If I could go in my house robe, I would." She laughed.

"How about that one?" I pointed at a dress that was a bit shoved to one side of the rack. "The lacy one? I always liked that."

"This? Oh, my. I'm not even sure I can fit into that one, anymore. Your dad always liked that one, you know?"

I ignored the remark about my dad. It had been ages since he and I had spoken, and I didn't want to deal with any extra emotions on a night that was already expected to be pretty emotional.

"Well, I like it," I said. "Give it a try. If it doesn't work, go for that sequined top and just pair it with some nice black pants and a low heel. Hair down. Just give it a good brush."

"What would I do if you weren't here?" she asked.

"Have a saner life," I answered, truthfully. "Listen, I love you, but I need to run and get changed myself. I have to meet Luke soon. See you there? Love you!" And I gave her a quick peck on the cheek.

"I'm proud of you honey, I really am," she said, calling after me.

"Mom, do *not* make me cry! My face will get all puffy. I'm outta here."

I bounded up the steps and into my room. I had laid out a few options on my bed. Luke and I have different tastes in clothes, so we weren't the types to discuss what we were wearing beforehand. There was no chance we would show up in matching outfits. I was *this close* to choosing a t-shirt with an obscure band name and a pair of comfortable ratty blue jeans, but I changed my mind at the last minute. I didn't want to wear a suit, and I'm not the tucked in button down shirt kind of guy, so I went with a black blazer, t-shirt and jeans. Very hipster, but hopefully not too played out.

"Barry?" I banged on the bathroom door. I could hear the shower running, but I couldn't hang around for him to finish before I left. "I need to run to Luke's. See you at the party later?"

"It's a date, Dolly!" he shouted through the door.

■ ■ ■

I was kind of on autopilot as I drove to Luke's place. At this point, Willie Nelson could probably drive himself there without much effort from me. My head was really out of it. Were we really about to have a fundraiser for social equality in my hometown? How did we get to this place? I was nervous as all get out, and I hoped there was something good in the future, and not scary. My head was swimming with a mixture of fear and optimism.

I parked the car and walked in Luke's door and could immediately smell his cologne. They say that out of our five senses, smell is the most linked to memory. Well, the scent of Luke Walcott was still enough to drive me wild.

"Babe, I'm here!" I called out as I headed down the hall to his bedroom. I caught sight of him standing in front of his bathroom mirror, trying to make the perfect knot in his tie. Khakis, Ralph Lauren Oxford cloth button down and brown leather loafers. The blue blazer was hanging on the doorknob. My weekend football hero in his traditional Southern uniform.

"Can you help me with this?" He was clearly frustrated. "I keep making it too short."

"Here," I said. "Let me do it. Your damn chest keeps getting bigger. You forget to compensate." I untied and retied it and the point landed perfectly at his belt line.

"You look great," he said, eyeing me up and down in the mirror. "Very New York. I like it."

"And you look like you're ready to go on ESPN."

"Now you're talkin'!" he smiled, then paused. "Are you ready for this?"

"Yeah, I think so. It should be pretty cool. Kit and Meredith are so excited. They haven't really shared so many details, but I trust them. Let's do it?"

"Let's do it." Kiss. Boom. Out the door.

■ ■ ■

Meredith and Kit did, indeed, go all out, and then some.

The evening was called "Love All." Simple, to the point, and without any hit-you-over-the head "gay agenda," so as not to scare some of the less vocal supporters away. I thought it was a perfect theme.

Since Luke and I had requested that no funds be raised for us specifically, the girls decided to partner with The Human Rights Campaign. The HRC set up a table just inside the door where donations could be collected for the general cause of equality in the state of Tennessee. I felt proud to be a part of that. The Supreme Court ruling for marriage equality was not the end of the struggle, and we knew that.

The gallery looked amazing. There were small bee lights strung up that crisscrossed the ceiling and then danced down the walls, between paintings, sculptures and other works of art. Votive candles artfully lit the surfaces. A bar was set up on one side serving cocktails, while waiters passed trays of champagne. There was a bandstand set up on the other side of the room with a microphone and instruments. It was early, but the small rooms were already filling up with supporters.

Kit and Meredith ran towards us as they saw us enter, champagne glasses in hand. Kit's wardrobe theme tonight was androgyny, and she was pulling off her Dietrich tuxedo with panache, top hat included. Meredith was all gold and sparkles and curves. Tommy and Shawn waved from the bar, drinks in hand. They were more than content to let their girlfriends have their moment to shine while they talked music.

"Well, if it isn't our men of honor! What do you think? *So. Good. Right?!*" exclaimed Kit.

"Ladies, you've outdone yourselves," I said. "First of all, you both look fantastic! And this is amazing. More than we could have ever imagined. Wait, are those Chesty Cheese pizzas?" A server was walking towards us with mini pizza slices on a silver platter.

"Yes!" Meredith was eager to finally tell me every detail. "We asked Peaches to donate some pies, and she was thrilled to be included. In fact, everything here is donated. Pizzas from Chesty Cheese, sushi from Saul's. The waiters and bartenders are from the Tater Tot. All the art featured tonight was donated to the cause and is being auctioned, and all the proceeds will benefit the Human Rights Campaign, as you requested. We even have a tattoo guy set up in the corner donating his time to make equality tattoos! But if you want anything non-gay, you have to pay for it." She frowned, as if anyone would make that choice.

"We're just starting with a little mood music," said Kit, "and then Shawn's band is playing, followed by a big surprise we have planned at the end."

"I don't know what to say. Honestly, I'm overwhelmed. Luke?"

"Kit, Meredith, I don't even know where to start," said Luke. "We're so grateful for your support. It just means the world to us."

"Oh, please," said Kit, top hat perched on the back of her head. "We *love* y'all. Now let's party!"

The night was a whirlwind of people coming up to us to wish us well, offer us drinks, even have their picture taken with us. It was very strange being a minor celebrity in Parkville. Luke was a bit more used to it, considering he was a former star athlete, but the reasons now were definitely new to him. He was coping quite well for someone who actually hadn't been out of the closet that long. We knew that Lana wasn't coming, of course, but I think he secretly hoped Red and Rosa would make a surprise appearance, even though Red had politely declined for the both of them. It was probably too much, too soon, and his father didn't want to appear to take sides, even though that's exactly what I thought he should do. But then again, it wasn't my family.

Speaking of family, I saw Mom pop in the door out of the corner of my eye as Luke and I were chatting with Saul and Rachel. She was alone. Where was Barry?

"Mom! Over here." I waved, and she came to join us, picking up a glass of champagne from a passing waiter along the way. "You wore the lacy dress!"

"It fit, after all," she said, posing with one hand at her hip. "I guess all that worrying about you has paid off."

"Happy to do my part," I teased. "You look great, Mom. Saul and Rachel, this is my mom, Audrey. They own Saul's Sushi. I've taken you there before, remember?"

"Oh, I love your restaurant!" Mom gushed. "The matzah ball egg drop soup is my favorite. I could eat that every day."

"Why, thank you," said Saul. "It's a pleasure to serve our customers here downtown. We love it. And we're happy to be here tonight. Rachel and I are honored to support these two. You know, we've been through a few fights ourselves. The good guys always win. You can count on it. Diversity is what makes this nation great." He pointed a finger up to the sky. "Now, we'll let you catch up with your wonderful son here. My wife and I have been eyeing those pizzas. They look delicious. Enjoy your night!"

"Where's Barry?" I asked, as Saul and Rachel made a beeline for the Chesty Cheese buffet.

"Oh, you know Barry. He still wasn't ready when I was, so he said to leave without him. He'll be along soon enough."

Shock the Monkey took the stage next, and Shawn and his band regaled us with a slew of awesome hits from the 1980s. Bammy and Michael were dancing next to me. Even though things were strained between us at work, I was so grateful that she had the courage to stand up for what she believed in, at least privately. As I scanned the room I felt like a teenager again, partying in my friend's basement, except tonight I was dancing with the hot football jock instead of myself, and I wasn't going home alone.

Luke leaned in to give me a kiss and no one really noticed, but if they did, they didn't seem to care. I was in heaven.

The band played their last song, and Kit came on stage to gather the crowd and make an announcement.

"Thank you, Shock the Monkey, for that awesome set! Let's give the band a great big hand, y'all! *Wasn't. That. Fun?* And isn't my boyfriend Shawn the cutest?" Shawn was wearing a tuxedo print t-shirt, to match his girlfriend. We all hooted and hollered, the champagne and drinks and dancing and heat all catching up with us. "But now it's time to move on to our main attraction of the evening. First of all, I'd like to thank Chesty Cheese, Saul's Sushi and the Tater Tot for donating their products and services tonight for a great cause. *Love! All!*" The crowd roared, and Luke and I roared right along with them. "Derek and Luke wanted this to be an evening centered around awareness, so we asked the Human Rights Campaign to be here tonight to answer any questions you may have, accept any donations, or even arrange for you to donate your time. They're set up right over there near the front door, so y'all be generous tonight, okay? But enough talk from me. Y'all want some more fun, right? Well how 'bout this? *Get. Ready!* Because Love All is pleased to present... the ladies of Chesty Cheese!"

The pop music started, and out came Tammy and the other ladies of Chesty Cheese, dressed appropriately for an all ages crowd, of course, but still covered in sequins and pasties and tassels. Peaches even came out of retirement to dance right along with them! They didn't have a stripper pole, but the show was as spicy and crazy as you'd expect, with lots of fake reveals and gymnastics. The crowd loved it. Even my mom was clapping along to the music. Tommy was doing that wolf whistle thing with his fingers. I never could figure out how to do that, myself.

The ladies ended their song with a can-can kick line. Very *Moulin Rouge*. The room went dark and a spotlight from the back of the room made its way from left to right along the line of dancers, then back left towards the center, where it focused on a new girl who had joined the line. She was a bit taller and had broader shoulders than the others.

No! It was Uncle Barry! But he wasn't Uncle Barry. He was dressed to the nines, as Beret! Long silver and white sparkling kaftan and a huge wig that crowded out the girls on either side of her.

I turned to my mom and she just blew me a kiss and winked at me. She must have been in on this all along! The can-can girls split the ranks, and Beret came forward, as the music segued into "I'm Coming Out," by Diana Ross. I was floored. Barry was coming out, big time.

"Wow," I said, almost to myself. "It's about time."

"Tell me about it," said Mom. I put my arm around her and we started dancing up a storm with the rest of my friends. Beret made her way down into the crowd and the lights got brighter, the music louder, and the people sweatier. It was an amazing moment of love, and I was overwhelmed. I was dancing with Beret, Mom was dancing with Luke, and we were surrounded by all of our friends. It was just too much.

"You're crazy, you know that!?" I screamed to Beret, over the pumping music that continued long after her set.

"What can I say? You inspired me, Dolly. It turns out you *can* teach an old queen new tricks. And besides, I'm too old to give a shit, anymore. If they don't like it, tough titties!"

"May I cut in?" I felt a tap on my shoulder. It was Mom. "I'd like to dance with my brother. He's too beautiful to pass up."

They embraced, and I took that as my cue to take a break. Luke was in a dance circle with Peaches, Kit, Meredith, and Tammy, and he looked like he was having the time of his life. I made my way to the bar to try and join Tommy and Shawn for a drink, but I couldn't find them, so I just asked for a sparkling water. From the time we had entered the building, Luke and I had been occupied with chatting, having our picture taken, grabbing a bite to eat, dancing and socializing. I hadn't had the chance to look around the room and see all of the beautiful works of art that had been donated for tonight's cause.

The girls had set up the art gallery rooms as silent auctions, so there were sign up sheets below each piece. Some of the paintings had already received bids for hundreds of dollars, and the night wasn't even over. There were oil paintings of lovers, nude and clothed, watercolors of beautiful sunsets and views from the lake. There were traditional paintings, modern art, everything.

But one particular piece drew my attention, and I walked over to take a closer look.

It was a modern art sculpture, constructed from rusted metal. This must be from the artist that Tommy had mentioned, the guy who uses pieces of rusted tractors and other farm equipment. I can see why Kit and Meredith wanted to represent him. It was beautiful. The sculpture was two hearts that were intertwined, extending triumphantly from a small pile of fused metal cogs and bars and assorted de-bris, as if they had climbed to the top of the mountain, together. I loved it. It really spoke to me.

I looked down at the auction sheet, and the highest bid was still within my reach. I decided I wanted it, but before I could sign the paper, I heard a voice behind me.

"You like it?" he asked.

"I love it," I said, looking up at the piece, and then turning my head to introduce myself.

I extended my hand and then saw his face. My smile turned south.

It was my dad.

10

HERE'S JOHNNY

I didn't know what to say. I couldn't speak. It was as if my brain and voice box had become disconnected from one another.

My mind was racing. I felt every emotion all at once, and nothing at all. My dad was standing in front of me for the first time in... so long that I couldn't even remember.

"Hi," he said, finally breaking the silence. "You look good."

"What?" I stammered. "What... are you doing here?"

He smiled nervously. "I wanted to help. I heard about what you were going through, and I just wanted to help. That's all."

"Help? Now?" I was stunned. "What the? Seriously? How the hell did you think you coming here would be a good idea?"

"Mr. Ray!" It was Meredith, over my dad's shoulder, walking towards us with a huge smile on her face. "Have you two met? Derek, this is Johnny Ray, the sculptor who we were so excited about. Isn't his work beautiful?"

Johnny Ray. His first two names. He must have dropped Walter when he dropped out of our lives.

"Excuse me," I said. "I need some air." I walked away as quickly as I could, leaving "Johnny Ray" and a confused Meredith in my wake, making my way through the crowd, still partying and celebrating love. I needed my mom. I needed to find her.

She was still dancing with Beret, where I had left her. I placed my arm on her elbow and said, "I need to speak to you. Now." She could sense something was up. Beret gave me a concerned look, but I ignored her and just walked straight through the front door, to the street. When I said I needed some air, I meant it.

Mom followed me through the doors and found me leaning up against the brick wall, underneath the soft glow of the downtown street lamps.

"Honey, what's wrong? What is it?"

"Did you know?" I asked, angrily.

"Know what?" Her face did not betray any deceit.

"Dad," I said. "Dad's here. Did you know?" I practically spit the words out.

She was silent, for a beat longer than I expected. Something was up. She exhaled, deeply.

"No," she said, finally. "I didn't expect him to be here tonight. I had no idea. But I'm not as shocked as you are. I didn't want to tell you, because I didn't want you to get upset. But he's been calling, lately. He reached out about a month ago, for the first time in years. We've been talking."

Of course. The phone calls. The hang-ups. That was him.

"I didn't have much to say, at first. But... he's Johnny," she said, by way of explanation. "He was always a charmer, you know? You get that from him."

"Great. Good to know," I said, sarcastically. "I guess I also got the gene that makes me want to run away from my problems. That was a great one to inherit. Go, genetics."

She was silent. I was fuming. Scared, angry, hurt, emotional. Everything.

"Does Barry know?" I asked.

"No, not yet. Barry and Johnny weren't on the best of terms when he left. You don't remember that, probably."

No, I didn't remember much at all about my dad, to be honest. When he was there, he wasn't really *there*, anyway. Then one day he was just gone, and it really didn't make that much of a difference in our lives.

Johnny Ray Walter was raised on a farm on the outskirts of Parkville, farther out west than Luke's parents' place. It was officially the next town, now, due to some land annexations. He attended Parkville High, like Mom and Barry, but today where he lived would be considered another school district. I didn't know much about their courtship, having pieced together small bits and details that I heard here and there as a kid. Mom and Dad had a mutual love of dancing, and apparently they would spent their nights twirling away at clubs, then head to the diner downtown near the university campus for late night breakfasts. That's how their romance started.

They were married quickly, right out of high school, both of them too young to realize that they weren't ready for the responsibility, and I was born just over a year later. Dad always had dreams of moving to the West Coast to pursue a career as an artist, but the obligations of his parents' farm, his wife and his only son kept him tied to Parkville. Later, when I asked Barry about my dad, he told me as politely as he could that Johnny just didn't like the expectations that were placed on him. In a way, he resented all of us for keeping him from his dreams. Mom and Dad started bickering, the marriage soured, and the fighting just escalated. I didn't notice anything, of course. I was too young. But one day, he just left. I wasn't even sure if they were ever officially divorced.

Years later when I was old enough to start caring, I asked where he was. Mom said he was somewhere in California, and we never really brought it up again. When his parents passed, I assumed he came home to pay his respects, but we never saw him. They had dropped out of our lives just as he had, for reasons I will probably never know. The property around the farm was sold to make way for a new subdivision, but the farmhouse remained, with a good parcel of land attached to it. It was a sad reminder of a time long forgotten, now surrounded by modern McMansions.

"What do we do?" I asked. "What am *I* supposed to do?"

"That's up to you, sweetie," she said. "If you want to talk to him, he's probably still here. Maybe you should hear him out? But that's up to you. That's your decision."

"I want Luke," I said, flatly.

"I'll send him out." She turned to go, then paused and turned back. "I love you. You know that, right honey?"

"I love you too, Mom." And she walked back inside to fetch my better half.

I couldn't be angry with her. He was her husband, after all. They had once been in love. Maybe they still were? If there was anything I did understand tonight, it was love. Love isn't always perfect and easy and proper, and it doesn't always follow your expectations.

I could almost feel my boyfriend's presence as he walked towards me. He placed his arms around me and said, "What's the matter, babe? Your mom said you needed me."

"It's my dad. He's here. I'm freaking out."

"Seriously? I thought he was pretty much out of the picture?"

"He was. He came back. The surprise party guest. My family likes a good entrance, remember?"

"Wow. What do you want to do? Should we leave?"

"Not until we go back inside, first," I answered. "This celebration is for us. It's our decision what happens next. I just... I don't know what to do. I need your help. I haven't spoken to him in years. What do I do, Luke?" I looked to his eyes for guidance.

He paused, in reflection. "Well, babe, my father and I didn't talk for years about the truths that were right in front of us. I regret that, but once I found the courage to fix it, I tried. Maybe this is your chance to fix your relationship with him? The theme for tonight *is* love, after all."

He smiled and his blue eyes bored into mine. I kissed him, softly, then punched him lightly in the center of his chest.

"Damn it, Mr. Right," I said. "How did you end up being such an even-keeled guy?"

"Sports. Taught me how to control my emotions. Every playing field is a new battle. Gotta stay focused." My warrior, always ready.

"Come on," I said, sighing. "Let's go meet Johnny."

We walked inside, hand in hand, as the party was winding down. My mom and dad were standing by his sculpture, talking. Barry was standing several feet away with a cocktail glass in his hand, looking at them warily. Luke and I walked up, and I introduced them. They shook hands and smiled, amiably.

"Listen," I said, "I don't really want to do this here. Can you meet tomorrow? How about the Tater Tot at noon? We can have lunch, just you and me."

"Sounds great," he nodded. "I'll see you there."

I gave Mom a kiss on the cheek and Luke and I turned to go, kissing and hugging our friends and new supporters along the way. It had been an amazing night, but I was emotionally exhausted. I wanted my bed, my man and a good night's sleep, if I could get it.

■ ■ ■

Dad and I met the next day at the Tater Tot at noon, as planned. He was already there when I arrived, and he had taken a table outside on the patio in the sun. I can't really say that I was nervous. My expectations were low. It just felt strange, more than anything else. My dad. Even saying that word felt foreign to my mouth.

"Good morning," I said formally, as I pulled out a chair and sat across from him. The patio was full, as usual. The Tater Tot was well known for its amazing brunch and weekend cocktail specials.

"Good morning, Derek," he started, warm but cautious, as he removed his sunglasses. Dressed in a t-shirt, lightweight linen pants and shoes with no socks, he looked very much the part of the California beach bum. "Thanks for coming out to meet me. I can imagine that this must feel a little odd to you. It's all new for me, as well."

Before I could respond, the waitress stopped by the table. "Can I get y'all some drinks to start with?"

"I'll have a Monster Mimosa, please," I said, looking up. "And keep 'em coming."

She smiled and made a note on her pad. "And you, sir?"

"Green tea with soy milk, please." She nodded and walked towards the bar. "I don't drink anymore, by the way," he said to me. "It clouded my judgment. Too many bad decisions."

"Well, a few more clouds aren't going to confuse me anymore than I already am," I said. "I hope that's okay for you?"

"Fine, fine." He nodded, unsure of what else to say.

We were stuck, already. This was awkward. Two grown men. Family. And no idea where to start.

"Listen," he began, "I didn't expect for you to run over here with open arms. I understand that. The only expectation I have for today is just for us to have a conversation, see where it goes. I know I made mistakes. I did. Plenty of them. And I can't make up for all the time I wasn't here. But if you'd give me the chance, I'd like to get to know you now, if I can?"

It was a statement and a question and a goal all rolled into one. He was trying. It really was my choice, what happened next. He was smart enough to know that it was up to me to make or break this. But I had to hand it to him. He finally showed up. And that took courage.

The drinks arrived and I let my mimosa work a little of its magic before I responded. He ordered the vegan falafel platter and an extra side of hummus. I ordered the cheeseburger with bacon and curly fries. We'd definitely chosen different paths there, but learning these idiosyncrasies was part of the adventure, and I made the decision to sign on for the ride.

"So," I said, giving in. "Where have you been all my life, stranger?" My Monster Mimosa had kicked in, apparently.

He smiled, catching the joke and took that as his cue. He started by recounting most of the stuff that I already knew. His and mom's courtship and subsequent marital breakdown were pretty much just how Barry had described it. A friend of his had moved out to Los Angeles, and when it seemed that nothing could go right for him in Parkville, he ditched it all and followed his friend to the West Coast, as he had always dreamed. He said that he knew leaving us was wrong, but he felt we would be better off without him. Starting over in a new town wasn't easy, but as my mom said, he was charming as hell, and it didn't take long before he had a pretty good life. He spent some time on a commune, became a certified yoga instructor, gave up meat and alcohol and smoking. He even studied Buddhism. It turns out that there was a freedom loving hippie on the inside just dying to get out, and discovering this turned his life around. He met a girl and they moved in together and she encouraged him to try his hand at art, as he had always wanted. He found out painting wasn't his thing, but when he starting sculpting from raw materials, everything just made sense to him. He caught a few lucky breaks and sold some pieces to a few prominent celebrities, and soon enough he had a following. Apparently he was now a fairly well known and respected artist. If I'd only bothered to Google him, I might have known that.

When his parents passed, one quickly after the other, he took care of all the details from a distance. He said he wasn't ready to come home. He'd made too many mistakes here, and this part of his life seemed so removed from his current path. He sold his parents' land, except for the farmhouse, deposited the money in the bank and kept working on his art. He and his girlfriend eventually split, amicably.

"And then one day I woke up and I was fifty years old. Fifty!" he said. "It's such a monumental number, you know. I was happy. Content. California's beautiful, but I suddenly realized it wasn't my home. Sure, the beach, the desert, the mountains, they're all beautiful. But that smog and all the driving? It was toxic. It took me two hours just to get anywhere, and I didn't want to end my life as a recluse, hiding on my compound, ordering everything online. I spent the next few years figuring things out. Before I blinked, I was fifty-five. Then I realized I didn't want to be there, anymore. I'd had a fun adventure, but it was time to come home. And that's when I reached out to your mom. Thankfully, she answered the call, and well, we just started talking again. I asked about you, and she told me about New York, that you had moved away, and then eventually returned home. Luke, the whole thing." He paused, taking a moment to really gather his thoughts. "I have a lot to atone for, Derek. I know that. But I'm not the man I was when I left."

I looked him straight in the eyes. "I believe you." He looked relieved. "Luke and I have this thing we do whenever everything goes wrong. We just hit reset. It goes something like this. *Hi, I'm Derek*." I extended my hand.

"Hi, I'm Johnny. Pleased to meet you."

"So, tell me about this sculpture I saw."

And we started again, from there.

11

BELLE, THE BEAST

The interim election for mayor took place on a Tuesday, as is customary, and Edward Bellman won by a landslide, capturing 100% of the vote. He was the only candidate after all, so the result was not unexpected.

What was unexpected, however, was his victory speech. For a man who did as little as possible as principal of Parkville High, he seemed to have discovered a fount of youthful energy in his new position, as he laid out a far-reaching plan to "clean up" Parkville and "save" it from its too inevitable crawl into the debauchery of the twenty-first century. This was a man, suddenly, who believed his own press. Family values? From the crossdresser? I wanted to laugh, but truly, I knew better than to be naive. As my grade school English teacher once taught us, "Power corrupts. Absolute power corrupts absolutely."

"That's Belle, for you," said Barry, as he scanned the *Parkville Post* that morning over his healthy breakfast of cantaloupe and cottage cheese. "I warned you she was a stage hog. Watch out, Dolly. I'm afraid you may be in her sights."

He was right. I should be worried. But I always believed that the right things would happen to the right people for the right reasons. Maybe I was a bit Zen, like my father, after all?

"Where's Mom?" I asked, reaching for a fresh made biscuit and slathering it with honey and butter. I was happy to see that we all weren't forced to follow Barry's strict carb-free diet.

"Out front, gardening," he said, looking up from his paper and peering towards the window. "She's taken to the yard, now that spring has sprung. She's also spending a lot more time outside with her phone, so I can't overhear her conversations."

"Ouch. We haven't really talked about that elephant in the room, yet. What are you thinking?"

He folded his newspaper, removed his reading glasses and looked at me pensively. "She's my sister. I'm protective of her, of course. But I think we lose our teeth a bit, as we grow older. Injustices from the past get cloudy, and we tend to forgive much more readily than we did in our youth. There's just not enough time in the world for anger. We learned that at your benefit the other night. Love all, right kid?"

"Well, maybe we should amend that to 'Love All, Within Reason?' You have more history with my dad than I do. I barely know the man. But I really feel like giving him a chance. Am I crazy?"

"Of course not," he said. "You don't have that shared history that we do. That's a blessing. Trust me. Start fresh and see what happens. But you'll understand if I'm a bit more cautious."

"Well, you weren't cautious on the stage the other night," I said, changing the subject. "You brought the boogie!"

"A girl's gotta do what a girl's gotta do," and he sipped his coffee as if it was just another day at the office.

"All right, Barry, I'm outta here. Time to face the fun." I finished off my biscuit and gave him a quick peck on the cheek. I was getting used to the morning ritual of walking past the protesters at school. Rather than be ashamed or intimidated, I tried to have as much fun with it as possible. It reminded me of *Steel Magnolias*. That which does not kill us makes us stronger, right?

The CCCP members had actually diminished a little leading up to the election, but after Mayor Bellman's fiery victory speech sparked the flames of animosity, their ranks were larger than ever. Most of the signs were harmless in their messaging, but other fringe members started to show up, and their slogans were downright hateful. It really pissed me off that they were angry with me for "exposing" their kids to homosexuality, while they were blissfully eager to expose those same kids to such vitriol and hate.

Remember that scene in *To Kill a Mockingbird* when Jem and Scout sneak out of the house at night and go to the jailhouse to see Atticus defending himself and his black client against an angry mob of would-be lynchers? The kids diffused the group by treating them like the friends and neighbors they were, and they shamefully dispersed on their own accord, embarrassed of their actions in front of innocent children.

Those days are long gone. Unfortunately, disagreeing in a respectful tone is a product of the past. It didn't matter that I greeted the protesters by name or commented on their outfits or attempted to instructively correct the horrid grammar on their signs, they simply wouldn't break a smile, no matter how hard I tried to make light of this awful situation. So much for levity.

Thankfully, Love All helped to organize some counter protests, and I was greeted with smiles and cheers from that group. Signs reading "Equality Now" and "Team Duke" helped to boost my spirits. I even spotted Saul and Rachel a few times, and I made sure to thank them, personally. I told them that I only hoped to feel as spritely as they do at their age. They assured me that I would, and I wanted to believe them, but the last few weeks had been difficult, for Luke, me, Bammy, and everyone in our circle.

Speaking of, Bammy sent me a text saying that she wanted to have lunch with me off campus, so I told her to meet me at Cochon's BBQ. She didn't have to say it, but I knew that it was better for her if we weren't seen leaving together. It felt like we were sneaking around. I hated what this was doing to our friendship.

Cochon's was a little barn wood smoke shack just over the county line. It had been there since I could remember, serving up the tastiest barbecued pork you've ever had, at a price everyone could afford. It wasn't fancy, but it was good, and that was all that mattered in these parts. I arrived before her, so I ordered two pulled pork sandwich platters with green beans, coleslaw, hushpuppies and two large sweet teas, with lemon. I claimed a spot on one of the old picnic benches by the big oak tree. Bammy showed up soon after, and I could tell by the distressed look on her face that she was either majorly stressed out or had some bad news to share.

"Oh, aren't you a doll ordering lunch? Next one's on me, okay?" she said as she sat down across from me on the rickety wooden bench.

"Will there be a next one?" I asked, unsure of what the look on her face meant. Was I about to be fired? Surely she wouldn't do that on a lunch date? I imagined the CCCP cleaning out my desk and the look of horror as they discovered my men's fashion magazines. "See! We told you!" I suppressed a chuckle.

"What are you talking about?" she said, as she dipped a hushpuppy in ketchup and popped half of it in her mouth. "Of course we'll have more lunches. It's just... Derek, I am *so* sorry. Really. This has been hard on everyone. Are you and Luke all right?"

"Yeah, we're fine," I said, stabbing my green beans with a white plastic fork. "It sucks not being able to have much contact with him at school, but in a way this has really pulled us closer together. Common enemy, you know?"

"I hope I'm not the enemy?" She frowned.

"No, Bammy. We love you. You know that. I know you're in a shitty place right now. They've tied your hands. I don't hold that against you."

She looked at me and I could see the tears welling up in her eyes. She put her sandwich down, and her whole face fell quickly into her hands.

"Bammy!" I reached for some white paper napkins and handed them to her to use as emergency tissues. "Honey, it's okay. Really! I understand. It's your job."

"It's not that," she cried, wiping her eyes. She was speaking so softly. "It's Michael."

"Again? Okay…" Now it was my turn to ignore my sandwich and concentrate on my friend in need. "What happened now? You two seemed great at the benefit the other night."

"We are," she sniffed, dabbing her eyes with the napkin. "He is. Great, I mean. But I… I. Oh, shit, Derek. I snooped." She threw her hands in her lap and looked at me, aghast.

My eyes grew wide. "Bammy? Are you saying what I think you're saying? The foster care paperwork? You didn't!"

"No! No, I wish. I mean, I *would* have, if I could have found it. He hid it, but good. Maybe even destroyed it. Oh, Derek, I watch too much TV. You know that! I couldn't find it, so I did the next best thing I could think of. I went onto his laptop… and I looked at his browser history. I thought it would help me. Give me a clue, you know? Oh, I wish I hadn't. He's done so many searches on the same person, over and over and over. It has to be him."

"Bammy, you're scaring me. Who is it?!"

"Your favorite and mine. Our new mayor. Edward Bellman."

"*No. Way.*" I was stunned. "Are you sure? Bellman?!"

"It was right there on his computer. Searches for everything. His career as a teacher. Where he lived. His family. Everything. That has to be it, right? Bellman is his dad."

"Holy shit. Are you *sure*, though? I mean, without the paperwork you're just guessing."

"Think about it, Derek," she reasoned. She had thought it all out. "Michael was born in August. School gets out at the end of May. Bellman was a teacher, then, before he became principal. He had summers off. He could have easily traveled away with his wife, had the baby, then come back and dropped him at the orphanage."

"Just like that. But why?" I asked. "Why would they hide that?"

"Maybe they couldn't afford to have a family?" she offered. "Maybe they weren't ready? Or they had marital problems? Or maybe they just didn't want kids, and Michael was an accident? Who knows?"

"Wow. Bellman. I think I just lost my appetite."

"Derek! That's awful!" But she started laughing, and so did I. We both needed a good laugh. Even an unexpected one.

"So what now?" I asked. "Will you confront him? And even so, what does this mean? Does this change anything?"

"I don't know," she said, hesitantly. "I have to think. If it's true, can we use this? Can this help you and Luke?"

I didn't know. This was all just too much at once. One thing was for certain, though. I reminded myself to change all my passwords. You never know who's looking over your shoulder.

"Bammy," I reasoned, "we can't use this unless it's true. We have to be certain. And even if it is, what would we do with it?"

"I don't know. Go to the *Parkville Post*? 'Mayor's Secret Lovechild?' That kind of thing? If we can take Bellman down, maybe this whole thing will just blow over?"

"No way, Bammy. No way. Think about what that would do to Michael. He'd be collateral damage. That's not fair. And putting aside your whole secondary gig as a secret spy, which I'm gonna overlook, you two have a good thing going."

"But if it would help you, Derek... I would." She looked wounded. Now I wanted to cry.

"Not gonna happen," I said, resolutely. "We'll find another way. Now eat your sandwich, Miss Talbot. We're gonna need our energy for the rest of the day. We'll figure a way out of this, but taking your boyfriend down in order to help me out is not on the list of possibilities."

■ ■ ■

I met my dad after school at Zen Yoga, downtown. I'd tried a few yoga classes in New York, but I was always so busy that I never had any real consistent time to devote to a practice. I wasn't sure that now was the time to start, with all the hectic things happening at school, but Johnny convinced me that I should give it a go. He said it would "align" me. Plus, he was looking for bonding experiences, and most of my ideas centered around drinking alcohol and eating fried food. I suggested jogging, but he claimed a knee injury, so here we were.

"Hey, Johnny," I said as I walked into the door of the studio. I was having a hard time calling him "Dad," and it kind of made me laugh to call him "Johnny," so it sort of just stuck.

He stood up from the couch near the reception desk and gave me a half man-hug and asked, "How was your day?" We took off our shoes and made our way into the main room. We grabbed two mats and placed them in the back towards the corner. If I was going to make a fool of myself, I figured I could at least try to hide my shame in the back row.

"Oh, you know. Same old, same old," I said, as I sat down on the mat and began my preliminary stretches. "Made my way through an angry mob with pitchforks, kids harassed me in class, Bammy dropped a bombshell at lunch, and now I'm hanging out with a man I haven't seen since I was too young to remember. Pretty standard, I guess."

He smirked. "Smart ass. You get that from your mother's side of the family." He was standing, trying his best to touch his toes and loosen his back.

"Derek! Hey there!" Tammy walked in the door with a group of girls from Chesty Cheese. Dressed in ripped t-shirts and short shorts that left little to the imagination, they placed their mats in the row in front of us. Tammy reached down and gave me a hug, exposing her best assets a bit too much. I thought Johnny's eyes were about to pop out.

"Tammy, this is Johnny. He's... my dad. Johnny, this is my friend, Tammy."

"The stripper," she laughed, as she offered him her hand. "Derek's just too polite to throw that part out there. But I kind of like the shock value of it, don't you?" She winked at him as she said it. She knew how to play to her audience.

"Oh, yes, most definitely," he said, taking her all in. "We said 'exotic dancer,' in my time. So how do you two know each other?" He pointed his finger back and forth, quizzically.

"Oh, Derek's a regular down at Chesty Cheese where I work. Y'all should come down some time! It's a blast. We'll see if Peaches has any father/son specials." She laughed and placed herself on the floor, stretching her legs before the class began.

Johnny looked at me, confused as hell.

"Yes, Johnny," I said. "I go to strip clubs. But I'm still gay. Not everything is so black and white."

"Oh, boy, do I have things to learn," he said, eyebrows high.

"Don't we all," I said. "Don't we all."

12

THE BONGO ROOM

"How was yoga?" Luke was in the kitchen making dinner when I arrived at his place.

"I feel like ten miles of bad road," I said, as I sprawled out on the couch. "That was not an easy journey. Apparently I'm not as stretchy as I used to be. We need to work on that."

He walked into the room, sat down next to me and handed me a glass of red wine.

"My hero! How'd you know I was at yoga, anyway?" I asked.

"You sent me a text. Don't you remember?"

"I send you lots of texts, smart ass. You never write back."

"That doesn't mean I don't read 'em." He smiled. "How's life with Johnny?"

"Strange, but interesting." I took a long sip of wine. "It's weird getting to know someone who you kind of already know because you share the same genes, but still, I don't really know him, yet. Oh, my god. You should have seen his eyes bug out when Tammy and the girls from Chesty Cheese joined us in class. He's definitely an admirer of beauty. For sure."

"Like father, like son?" He looked at me, playfully.

"Are you flattering yourself, Coach?"

He laughed. "What are you up for tonight? Dinner will be ready in about twenty minutes. A quiet night on the couch? Movie?"

"You know what?" I said, and placed my almost empty wine glass down on the coffee table. "We need something to take our minds off all this BS for awhile. Kit invited us to see Shawn's band at the Bongo Room tonight. How's that sound?"

"That sounds perfect. I need something to distract me from my family. I just hung up the phone with my father."

"Uh oh. Trouble with Red?"

"No, not really," said Luke, picking at the shiny paper label on the neck of his beer bottle. "At least, I don't think so. I think he feels the need to intervene. Family patriarch, and all. He's invited us over for a family dinner on Friday. Lana, you and me. All of us. It was a positive move from him, that's for sure, but if I was a betting man I'd say it was Rosa's idea."

"Well, it doesn't matter whose idea it was," I said. "Let's hope we can solve everything, because if not, I think you and I need to consider the Witness Protection program. I'm thinking France."

"Perfect solution, Mr. Runaway, but right now let's stick with your plan of drinks and music."

"Spoil sport. You'd look so good in a blue and white striped t-shirt and a beret."

■ ■ ■

The Bongo Room was downtown in the Warehouse District. We called it "the WD," which actually sounded more like "the Dubbya Dee." In the early 1900s the railways extended themselves through the more populated Southern towns, and Parkville made the grade. The WD quickly established itself as the center for trade and commerce. When the railroads began to die out, so did this part of town. The warehouses were emptied and abandoned and became derelict husks of the thriving centers they once were. The drifters and the taggers started breaking down the doors and claiming their territory, and soon the area became pretty dangerous, by Parkville standards. Then, in the early 90s, young artists and musicians who lived near the university felt they were being priced off campus due to rising housing costs, so they started buying up the lots and buildings in the WD for next to nothing. Gentrification happened quickly, and suddenly Parkville had a new thriving arts community downtown. Warehouses became loft condominiums, coffee houses appeared on every corner, and bars and nightclubs sprang up to give the local residents some entertainment. All they needed now was a fancy health food store, and there was a rumor that one was on the way.

The Bongo Room was one of the early pioneers in the WD, just over one hundred years after the warehouses were built. A group of local musicians were looking for a performance space, and they found the perfect building. They made some inquiries, and it turned out they were able to buy it for a song. Literally. The former owner suggested a price that was more than fair, but the musicians weren't able to pool as much money as they needed, so they threw a musical benefit for their own cause. The proceeds from the door were enough to cover the funds they lacked, and the Bongo Room was born.

The front room was long and narrow, with a bar on the right and a staircase on the left leading up to another floor that was used for offices, sound studios and living quarters. Beyond that, the back room was a performance space with hardwood floors, brick walls and a bandstand along the far wall. When the temperatures were really flying high in the summer, they would open the sliding emergency exit doors along the back wall to create a cross breeze, and occasionally the whistle of a single train running along that one remaining ghostly track would add a new layer of eerie music to the pounding beat within.

My friend Aisha was working the front door that night. Her real name was Amy, but she changed it in college because she said it sounded too white, and besides, who ever heard of a black girl named Amy? We're all allowed to create our own identities, right?

"Hey, Aisha! You look great. You always do." I gave her a hug.

"You too, sweetie," she said. "You know, I always wondered why people don't dress like every night is Friday night. The world would be a whole helluva lot prettier."

She snapped the fingers of her left hand. "Y'all can come in for free, by the way. I heard about all that nonsense they're putting you through and I'm rootin' for y'all."

"We wouldn't think of it," I said, smiling. "Luke? Pay the woman. She's handing out compliments. I'll go get us some drinks."

"Shawn and the rest of them are already inside," she said, pointing towards the back. "Have fun, y'all!"

I heard the music from the next room. Shawn's band wasn't up yet, and I spotted the Scooby Gang at a round table opposite the bar. Tommy had his arm around Meredith and Kit and Shawn were obviously cracking each other up over something.

"Is there room for two more?" I asked, as we approached the table.

"Yay!" said Kit. "*Love. Love. Love!*" She jumped up from the table and gave me a big hug and a kiss on the cheek.

"Why don't you do that when you see me?" asked Shawn.

"Derek doesn't make me do dishes, baby." We all laughed.

They scooted around the table and Luke pulled up an extra chair. Meredith looked at me like she was a bit nervous to speak and I cocked my head, quizzically.

"Derek, I need to apologize to you." She was so sincere. Almost timid.

"What for?" I asked.

"Well, I didn't know about Johnny Ray. That he's your dad. Kit, either. We just loved his art and felt like he would be perfect for the Love All benefit, but if we had known…"

"Meredith, there's no need for an apology." I needed to put her at ease. "There's no way you could have known. None of you had ever met the man. And honestly, you made the right choice. His art was perfect. He's the one who pulled one over on you."

"Duplicity. Mischief. There are a few more traits you share." Luke winked at me.

"Watch it, Coach," I warned him. "You never know what tricks I may have up my sleeve. Anyway, I'm glad Johnny was there. We're trying to get to know each other now, and that wouldn't have happened if y'all hadn't thrown that benefit. Cheers!"

Clinking bottles and glasses, all around.

"How's business, Tommy?" said Luke, changing the subject. For a handsome man, he was not so at ease being the center of attention, and it seemed all anyone wanted to talk about lately was us. Tonight was supposed to be about taking a break from that.

"Pretty good. Can't complain," he said. Tommy's the kind of guy who sees the good in every situation. "I'm actually doing some work at Amber's place, out by the lake. I'm pretty sure she made some serious bank after that third divorce. She has me extending her deck and upgrading the hot tub. I can do a shitty job, if you want me to?" he joked.

"Nah, she worked hard for that money," said Luke. "We all saw those husbands, right?"

"Let's be honest. Any guy she chose after you was a downhill decision, babe," I said.

"It's show time, y'all," said Shawn, rubbing his hands together. "I need to set up. Ready to get your groove on?"

"Hell, yeah!" said Kit and we picked up our drinks and pushed our way through to the back room, claiming the front of the stage. We were Shock the Monkey groupies, and we were ready to rock and roll!

An hour later we were soaked through with sweat and our faces hurt from grinning. I had screamed so many lyrics that my voice sounded like a mix between Lauren Bacall and James Earl Jones. The band always ended their set with a Tennessee favorite, updated to today's sound. Tonight's final song was a funky remix of *The Tennessee Waltz*, and we all waltzed and schmaltzed our way from one corner of that dance floor to another, stepping on toes and taking names like we owned the place. By the time it ended, I was truly exhausted, but it was worth every minute of fun. We certainly needed it.

"Take a break outside with me?" Luke asked.

"We'll see y'all in a few minutes," I said to our friends. "Grab a table? We're just getting some fresh air."

We stepped out back through the emergency exit doors, past the security guard. We went to high school with him, of course, but I couldn't remember his name. He let us pass with just a nod. With two red plastic cups full of water to rehydrate us, we sat out on the fire escape overlooking the train tracks and quietly enjoyed the stillness of the night. The air was much cooler outside, and it felt so good to be free from the oppressive humidity on the dance floor.

"Why so serious, Coach?" I could see it on his face. But this had to happen, eventually. I try to coast through all the crappy parts of my life with humor, but all of this was new to Luke. He'd had a pretty carefree life before I showed up and brought all the drama. Now he was dealing with coming out, family squabbles, problems at school. He smiled through it all, but it had to take its toll, eventually.

"I've been thinking, about what you said earlier. Witness Protection."

"Babe, I was kidding! We're not moving to France. I could never eat all those carbs."

"I know we're not moving," he said. "But be serious, just for a moment. What happens if we have to quit? Or if we get fired? What are we going to do? Coaching is who I am."

"I don't know," I said, truthfully, shaking my head. "I hadn't really thought that far. I'm kind of impulsive, you know? I just try and go with the flow. I'm Blanche DuBois, relying upon the kindness of strangers."

He turned to look at me, eyes narrowing. "Tennessee Williams?"

"You're learning, grasshopper." I smiled, but he still wasn't happy. "Seriously, Luke. I don't know. We'll have to face it when it happens. But we'll face it together, okay? I have no doubt we'll land on our feet."

"But what if we don't?" I'd never seen him like this. Unsure of himself. "I know I'm getting ahead of myself, but... we may want kids someday, Derek. If we want to be a family, we need to make choices that can support that, emotionally and financially."

I held my breath for a second. I wasn't ready for this.

"Luke, I..." I just looked at him, blankly. "We'll have plenty of time to figure that out. Right now, I can barely take care of myself. Of us. I mean, I may want a dog some-day, but that will mean I can't run off whenever I want. I haven't even *considered* kids. I have no clue what the future holds for us. I just know I want to be with you, but I can't think too far ahead, you know?"

"You make me feel like anything is possible, you know that?" he said.

"That's the sweetest thing you've ever said to me." I kissed him softly, under the moonlight on a fire escape in the WD. The teenager in me was still alive, jumping up and down inside. But that conversation about kids would have to wait for another day.

"Now come on. Let's head back inside before they think we ghosted," I said.

He stood up, and then held out his hand to help me. We walked past the security guard again and made our way back to the front bar. The gang had commandeered a new, larger table by the front window, and Tammy and Scooter had joined them. That was a nice surprise.

"Well, lookee there, if it isn't Parkville's resident gay activists," said Scooter, smiling wide and showing off a wad of chewing tobacco between his cheek and gum.

"Shut up, Scooter," said Tammy, giving him a playful whack with her hand. "They're my friends. Give 'em a break, will ya?"

"Aw, hell, I'm just kidding. Luke and I played football together in high school. Shoot, if I'd known then what I know now, maybe I woulda given you more of a show." He laughed.

"Trust me, Scooter," said Luke, knowingly. "You weren't my type and I wasn't looking."

"Aw, hell, I'm just givin' y'all grief, you know that. I think it's kinda stupid that the town is all freaked out over this. Who gives a rat's ass? Y'all are two upstanding dudes, in my book. Y'all have my vote." And he raised his beer bottle, in salute. That meant a lot, coming from a backwoods guy like Scooter.

"Besides, anyone with half a brain knows what this is really about. Them kids couldn't give a flying Frisbee what y'all do in your bedroom. They're just havin' fun. Hell, remember those bomb threats we used to have in high school? Spring semester our senior year we musta had 'bout ten of 'em. Those were the best, weren't they? We all got to leave early and we'd just head on down to the lake to party. Man, those were good times," he said, reminiscing.

"Scooter!" I practically spit my beer out at him. "You're a genius! I could kiss you!"

"What'd I say?"

"Babe, we can't call in bomb threats. That's a felony," Luke said, concerned. "I'm not ready to go to prison for something like this."

"No, not that!" I was so excited I could barely speak. "Luke, we gotta go. Now!"

Everyone was looking at me like I was crazy, but it all suddenly came together in my head. I reached across the table and laid a big, wet sloppy kiss on Scooter's cheek. His face turned redder than a Bama fan on game day, and Tammy about busted a gut she was laughing so hard. I grabbed Luke's hand and yanked him up.

"Hurry up! Let's go!" I practically shrieked. "We have calls to make."

13

THE FIRE WENT WILD

I could barely sleep Thursday night, my head was spinning with all the what ifs. I was pretty sure we had planned for every possible outcome, but if we had set the dominos up correctly, there was really only one way they could fall.

We decided to head to work together in Luke's car, defiantly. It was important to really plant our feet firmly today if everything was going to go according to plan. He parked the Jeep in the teachers' lot and we walked right past the CCCP protesters, holding hands. It was a simple message, and this gesture was enough to really set them on fire.

The Love All crowd cheered us on as we approached them. We shook their hands and thanked them for their efforts. We had placed plenty of calls the night before and rallied the troops, and our side was visibly larger today than the CCCP. Saul and Rachel were there, most of the staff from the Bongo Room and the Tater Tot, and Peaches brought out the whole crew from Chesty Cheese in their finest Daisy Dukes and bikini tops. If we were going to have reporters show up, we wanted them to interview as many people as possible from our side, and let's face it, sex sells.

Luke and I walked up to the front doors of the school and turned to face the crowd, raising our hands together in unity, as if we were a political couple entering the White House. In a way, this was a political gamble. We were really rolling the dice, though. One well-placed chip could pay off, but an unlucky hand could end our careers altogether. Sometimes you have to bet it all to win big.

We entered the school and he flashed that winning grin. "Break a leg, Mr. Walter," he said.

"Give 'em hell, Coach."

I walked by the first floor office and gave Miss Mabel a nod through the glass wall. She hadn't said much to me throughout this whole ordeal, but I could feel her eyes on me more than usual, lately. She was starting to look up more. I wondered if she thought I was brave or foolish, considering her own choices in life. It's a different world, Miss Mabel. Not only is there no need to stay closeted, but truthfully, no one cares anymore. Your friends will stand by you, and the rest are free to make their own choices, but we can all get along fine if we just try. Our politics don't need to agree 100% for us to remain friends. We just need to stand up for fairness and equal treatment. But without people like Miss Mabel, Aunt Janey and Uncle Barry, I wouldn't have the courage to be who I am today. I reminded myself to ask her out to lunch when this is all over. I'm sure she has some great stories to tell, if she's willing.

The world had, indeed, changed a lot since Bellman and Miss Mabel came to work at Parkville High. Schools used to be a place of education, halls were filled with students eager to learn their history, acquire math skills, pick up foreign languages, improve their social skills and become physically fit. Somewhere along the way that changed. Social media, selfies, the twenty-four hour news cycle and celebrities who were simply famous for being famous contributed to a new, evolving atmosphere. Sure, some students were still there to learn. Knowledge is power, after all. But for the most part, school became a holding tank, and teachers began to feel more like wardens and less like educators.

Public schools are funded by the government and have budgets like any other business. That's an important fact to remember. A school is a business, and a business has to make money to survive. As education cuts were enacted, the vending machines paid their way into the party and replaced the once healthy meals. The playing fields and uniforms were branded with corporate sponsors, and every kid who attended school equaled another coin added to the accounts ledger for the business. As a teacher, the first task on my daily to-do list was to take attendance, because more bodies equal more money, and schools really, really needed the money.

"All right kids, let's get started," I said as I entered my first period class. "If you could all take your seats, please. Thank you."

The room quieted down, and there was a noticeable tension in the air. Something was up, and everyone could feel it. Eyes darted left and right, as if they were waiting for the bravest one among them to make the first move. It was *Lord of the Flies*. Who would throw the first spear?

"Okay," I said slowly, testing the waters. "Let's start with attendance."

"Wait." A voice broke through the air. It was soft, at first, but insistent. Then silence. I looked up to see who had spoken.

Jett stood up from his desk, a nervous smile on his face. I looked concerned, and he could see that. A wicked grin quickly replaced his nerves.

"You'll have to count me absent, Mr. Walter," he said, with a newfound air of confidence. "My mom doesn't want me in this environment anymore, and I have to agree with her. This just isn't the place for a young, impressionable kid like myself." He picked up his backpack and stood there for a moment, waiting. Would anyone back him up?

"Me, too," said a buddy of Jett's. "Count me absent." He stood as well, and together they started to walk towards the classroom door with their things.

"I'm sorry, Mr. Walter." It was one of my theatre kids, standing at his desk, too. "It's not my choice. It's my parents. They're making me." And he gathered his belongings and walked slowly towards Jett, fully projecting his awareness of the pain he knew his actions would cause me.

Within minutes, the entire classroom was standing at the door. Jett, the Pied Piper of Parkville High, led them from the room, where they joined hundreds of other students, already roaming the halls towards the main entrance.

I stood there in my empty classroom and looked at the desks, reflecting on what had just happened.

And I started laughing.

■ ■ ■

They say those raging wildfires that devastate California in the dry seasons are started by a lonely spark, usually an errant match or dying cigarette, casually tossed by a passerby.

Jett was our spark, and after him, the fire went wild.

When the entire student body of a high school walks out en masse, you can bet your ass every local news team will show up to report on the chaos. It wasn't long before the national teams showed up, too, and suddenly we had a raging firestorm of a story.

Bammy was out front and center, leading the charge for the school. That was her job, after all, to defend the school board and to defend the mayor, all the while straddling that fine line between parents' rights and the need for the students to return to classes. She was polite and erudite, without resorting to name calling or appeasements to the more lowbrow residents who were surely watching her every move. It was a difficult performance, and she pulled it off with grace.

Luke and I stood united with a bay of cameras and reporters facing us, prepared with a simple statement focused on equality, our legal rights, and our combined and determined focus on simply returning to work, as soon as possible. Our message was clear. We were not the ones standing in the way of these children's educations. The parents were.

As principal, Bammy had no choice but to shut the school down for the day, as well as the foreseeable future. The students made it very clear to every camera and news reporter who would listen. They would not be returning to school as long as their parents told them to stay home.

I caught Bammy's eye as she gave her umpteenth interview for the day. She did her best not to notice me, but I could see the strain. This was tough on her, but she was doing great. Her cell phone rang, and she turned to excuse herself. It was a call she had to take. She spoke quietly on the phone, then turned back to announce that she had just received a call that there would be an emergency school board meeting that night, a closed session to discuss their next move, privately. She thanked the reporters for their time, then reentered the school, followed by a trail of paparazzi.

■ ■ ■

Luke and I worked the crowd and made sure our message was received loud and clear by all the reporters and cameramen present, then we left in his car and headed to the gallery, otherwise known today as Love All Headquarters. "Operation Walkout" had been a huge success.

"*Shit*," I said, once we were safely ensconced in his vehicle and I was sure we were no longer being recorded. "Shit! Shit! Shit! Shit! Shit! I can't believe that worked. I'm freaking out!"

"Let's just hope it continues to play out as we planned, babe," said Luke, shifting gears and getting us the hell out of there. "Tell me what happened! Who stood up first? Was it Jett, like we thought?"

"Yes! Of course. He's a born leader," I said. "He wants everyone to follow him. You can see that. My poor theatre kids. I felt so sorry for them. They were all prepped to go first, just in case, but it was exactly like you said. They hesitated, just like we asked them to, and Jett took over. He took the bait. Suddenly someone else's plans for a coup were his. You should have seen the smirk on his face!"

"It was the same in my first period PE class. Chip stood up first. I'm not even sure he ever sat down. He just walked straight in, announced he was leaving and walked straight out, with everyone else following. He and Jett must have discussed it last night. They really think they're in control of this thing, don't they?"

"They do," I said, excitedly. "But it's not a home run, yet. Waddya say we try and steal third, today?"

"Are these sports metaphors just for me? 'Cause you're turning me on."

"What can I say? You must be influencing me."

"I'd say that's mutual."

We arrived at the gallery and entered to cheers from Kit, Meredith and the many supporters who had gathered to watch the live news feed on the television they had hooked up for the day on the 52" digital art screen. Not everyone was completely on board with what just went down, so we thought it best to bring the group up to speed.

"Hey, y'all," I began, "thank you so much for being here today to support us. It means the world to Luke and me. 'Operation Walkout' was a huge success, and we want to catch you up on the details right now. Basically, schools are paid by the government based on attendance, per student, per day. It's all about the money, right? So, thanks to a little nugget casually tossed off by our friend Scooter, we came up with a fantastic plan. If all the students walk out, then the school gets no money. We have a theory that the kids could care less that we are gay. Basically, they just want out of school. So we played on that. With a few well-placed phone calls to some of my trustworthy theatre students and Luke's loyal athletes, we initiated the idea for a walkout. And we were lucky enough that the idea not only caught on, but that the social leaders of the school took on the plan as their own. We wanted a walkout, and boy, we got a walkout!" The gallery erupted in cheers.

"But here's the thing," I added, cautiously. "Right now, we control the narrative. The story is still anti-Derek, anti-Luke." The cheers became boos. "No, no, no," I responded, "it's cool. Because together, we're gonna change that. Here's what we're counting on. We're pretty sure the school board will suspend us, and that's fine. That's okay. But we're also pretty sure that the students won't go back to school, even if we're not there. They're counting on some holiday time, right? So, let's say that there is a suspension."

As if on cue, my cell phone rang. I looked at the screen and saw that it was Bammy. I held my hand up, and asked the room for silence.

"Bammy!" I answered, cheerfully.

"Mr. Walter?" She was cold, sterile. "Hello, this is Principal Talbot calling. Do you have a moment to speak?"

"*Whoa*," I said, immediately understanding. "I take it you're at the school board meeting?"

"Precisely, Mr. Walter. It's my duty to inform you that regrettably, the school board has handed down a unanimous decisions to suspend you and Mr. Walcott for one week, pending a public hearing on Friday."

"Got it," I said. "Call me later when there aren't others watching your every move?"

"Thank you for understanding, Mr. Walter. I assume you will communicate the same message to Mr. Walcott? I will pass on the message that you have accepted our ruling. We will see you next Friday at 7pm. Good day to you, sir." And she hung up.

Wow. I knew that was tough for her, but I was so proud of my Bammy. She was playing her role to a T, and she was nailing it.

"That was Bammy. Principal Talbot, I should say. Luke, we've been suspended for a week." Again, more boos. "But!" finger pointing in the air, "there will be a public hearing next Friday at 7pm. And that, my friends, is our deadline. Our last shot. We need to turn this story around, and we have seven days to accomplish that. This isn't a story about closed-minded teens who are afraid of gay teachers, this is a story about closed-minded *parents* who are afraid of their kids growing up and experiencing the real world. And whatever parents don't like, kids love, am I right? If those kids want to really piss off their parents, we need to help them refocus their message. They won't go back to school unless Luke and I *are* there, teaching and coaching just as we did before this whole mess started. Can I get an AMEN?!"

I had never felt so much like a preacher in my life, standing in front of that growing, cheering crowd. I was trained as an actor, sure, so public speaking came easy to me, but I had found a passion that I never knew could exist in me like this. It was love. And I was doing all of this because of the love of my fantastic friends and the amazing man standing by my side.

"Derek, it's Tommy!" Meredith was yelling to me from the back of the room, cell phone in her hand. "He was just at Amber's place, working. He said he has something he needs to tell you and he's on his way here."

■ ■ ■

Tommy stood with me, Luke, Meredith and Kit in the corner of the gallery. I was pretty sure he had broken every speed limit from Amber's place to downtown, because he showed up in record time.

"So, I was over at Amber's today," he began. "Like I told y'all, I'm working on extending her deck. You know what it's like. I'm running around, minding my own business, and they don't even really notice I'm there. I'm 'the help,' you know? I'm invisible. Anyway, Jett shows up because school has been cancelled, and he starts to tell Amber the whole thing, like it was his idea to stage a walkout, when you and I know y'all basically fooled him into doing it. So Amber props him up and is all proud of him and shit, like he did a great thing. Seriously, these two are like best buds. She doesn't even try to parent him. But long story short, y'all were right. He doesn't give a shit that you're gay. For him it's all about just not going to school. He straight up told her that. And Amber? She doesn't care, either. For her it's all about revenge." He turned to Luke. "I don't know what you did to her, Luke, but that woman hates you. Or she loves you? Kinda both, actually. Whatever, she just wants to see you suffer. How'd I do?"

"Sweet!" I said. "Best spy ever!" Meredith gave him a great big hug. He was definitely getting lucky, tonight.

My phone buzzed again, and I pulled it out of my pocket. Bammy.

"Derek!" I could hear her heart pounding through the phone.

"Bammy! Can you talk, now?"

"Derek, I'm so sorry! But I had to. You know that. I feel just awful."

"Bammy, slow down," I said. "Take a breath. Everything's cool. You did great! I was so proud of you."

"I was 'bout to die," she drawled. "Talking out against you practically killed me, but I stuck to the high road. They fell for it, just like you said they would. I stood in line, just like a good soldier. They wanted to fire you and Luke on the spot, but I talked them out of it. Michael and I, both. Talk of lawsuits and legal battles and national press focus on the town, and they fell in line just like we wanted them to. No one wants all that negative attention. We have one week, my friend. One week. I hope you have the rest of this plan figured out, because if you don't bring the big guns to that school board meeting on Friday, it looks like we're cooked."

"So far, so good," I said, "but yeah. Still some pieces to figure out. Red has asked us to dinner tonight at his place. He's trying to mediate an end to the animosity between Luke and Lana. But we can't let him in on our real reasons for what happened today, so we just have to play along.

And honestly, Lana is our Plan B. She has the power to call off the CCCP. She may still be our best bet. Wish us luck?"

"Good luck, my friend," she said. "I love you. I would not go through this nonsense for anyone else, you hear me?"

"Loud and clear."

"Today was pretty nerve racking," she said, her voice quavering. "Michael's taking me to dinner tonight. He's acting all sketchy. I'm not sure my heart can handle anything else today. Either he's found out that I snooped and he's gonna tell me off, or he's just tired of me asking so many damn questions and he's gonna tell me everything. Regardless, I'll text you later. Love ya, bye."

Operation Walkout, over and out.

14

THE WALCOTTS

I was admittedly nervous heading over to meet Red and Rosa. I'd heard so much about them from Luke, and of course I had accidentally discovered Red at the Bears' Club in Beret's dressing room, though I quickly pretended not to see them together. We had yet to be formally introduced though, and tonight I wasn't invited just as a friend; I was to be presented as Luke's boyfriend. I felt like a debutante at a coming out ball. Yikes. There was so much that could go wrong tonight, and I had to be on my best behavior. Unfortunately I know myself, and when I get nervous, I drink. And when I drink, I get chatty. And when I get chatty, I say stupid things. Luke quietly reminded me to watch my intake of alcohol. I could easily have been offended, but when he's right, he's right.

The Walcotts were Parkville's answer to *Dynasty*. Red Walcott was Blake Carrington. Not John Forsyth, the actor who played Blake, but Blake himself: a nattily dressed silver haired fox who had his pick of the ladies when he was younger, and could probably do the same today. That Walcott charm goes far, and both Luke and Lana inherited his infectious smile, whether it was backed with good intentions or simply being used as a persuasive tool. Ever the salesman.

Red made his fortune in land deals, or as Rosa would say later during dinner, "He sells dirt." He certainly didn't have a rough start in life. Red's grandfather and father had been involved in local business as far back as anyone could remember, making deals and establishing Parkville as an important trade stop between the North and South. The railroads, the Warehouse District, urban planning, the Walcotts had been involved in it all, and they had profited enormously. Red took his father's inheritance and invested in land. He flipped properties, pushed for rezoning and deregulations, and helped to create sprawling commercial shopping centers where farms and pastures once reigned supreme. He didn't just sell dirt; he sold dreams to prospective buyers. And they made him rich by buying it all.

Uncle Barry had told me that Red was naturally expected to marry Posy. Sure, he played the field, but they both knew that neither of them had a choice, eventually. Theirs wasn't a romance for the ages, it was more a romance for the pages. The Parkville society pages, to be precise, had proclaimed their match a done deal, and they simply needed to follow through with it, no questions asked. You could say they were in the same weight class.

Posy Walcott, née Lindbergh (no relation to Charles, but how kind of you to inquire), also had an electric smile, but hers was made of glass, unmoving. Some say she inherited her cold nature from her Scandinavian ancestors. She was ice. Beautiful, glistening ice. A member of every charity board, the head of every social club, Posy established her rule quite quickly, and no one dared lay claim to her throne. She was untouchable.

Unfortunately, that very same nature that kept her onlookers at bay also extended to her two children, Luke and Lana.

We approached the front door and Luke reached out to ring the doorbell.

"It's the house you grew up in," I said. "Can't we just walk in?"

"Welcome to the Walcott residence," he said, back straight, eyes forward. "There are rules, and rules are meant to be followed."

"Shit. What have you gotten me into?"

"You said that out loud, you know?" We could hear footsteps approaching. "Inside voice, remember?" He gave my hand a reassuring squeeze.

You know that feeling when you are in the first car of the roller coaster, and the wheels beneath you are *clicking* and *clacking*, ascending their way up to the very peak of the track before that first death-defying drop? The excitement is building, and you know the ride will either be awful or amazing, but you kind of wish you could just get off and have your friends tell you about it later so you can make up your mind based on their experiences? Yeah, that. Times ten. That's what I was feeling right now. Honestly, I was trying so hard not to pass gas.

"*Mijo!*" a voice cried out. It was Rosa, welcoming Luke into her outstretched arms. She was everything I expected, but not quite what I had pictured in my mind.

Short, but not as round as I had imagined, she was petite and soft and a little flashy. Dark curly hair, with perhaps a few too many jangly bracelets, she was dressed with style in mind, but a greater nod to comfort than one would imagine Posy would have favored. She had been employed by the Walcotts since Luke's birth, and you could instantly see the bond those two shared, her bright red lipstick lingering on his cheek. I immediately wished I had met her earlier.

"Come in! Come in!" she said, closing the door behind us as we entered the grand foyer. There was an imposing, winding staircase just behind her to the right. On our left, a set of ancient wooden pocket doors were rolled back to reveal an opulent sitting room. The pocket doors to our right were closed to what I assumed was the dining room, the setting of this evening's dinner.

"Let me a take a look at you, *mijo*!" She held his arm out, almost as if she expected him to pirouette in her hands. She looked him up and down, beaming. "Staying in shape, I see. Such a handsome man you are. Are you eating enough? I'm sending you home with tamales. Don't give me that carb nonsense, okay? I don't want to hear it from you." There was no doubt who was in charge here.

"And you," she said slowly, giving me a serious look with one raised eyebrow and a distinct lack of enthusiasm. "You must be Derek." Pause. Oh, shit. I'm on deck. Man up, Walter.

"Yes," I said, forcing a nervous smile and finding my voice. "It's a pleasure to meet you. Luke has told me so much about you."

"Oh, really?" she said, letting a smile slowly form on her face. "Well, we don't know enough about you, yet. I hope you're ready for the Mexican Inquisition?"

I smiled, gamely, and glanced at Luke. Help?

"I'm just playing with you!" she said, and she and Luke started laughing. "Welcome to our home." She pulled me into her arms and her hug was warm and soft and I detected a whiff of cinnamon. It was a comforting gesture, and she made me feel a little more at ease. But not too much.

"Your father is in the library," she said, pointing a finger down the hallway. "He's expecting you. I have some things to finish in the kitchen. Go ahead, I'll be in later."

The library. The dining room. The parlor. The veranda. The rooms in the Walcott residence had names. I was in a real life game of Clue. Situated high on a hill at the west edge of town, it overlooked acres of undeveloped land that was once used for farming and horse pastures. It had been modernized since it was built after the era of Reconstruction, but it still maintained its distinctive Southern character. This was dirt Red would never sell.

Luke led the way as we walked down the long hallway, passing more rooms with names and purposes I could only imagine. I felt like an intruder, albeit an invited one.

The library was situated at the back of the house. Double tall in ceiling height, there were three walls filled voluminously with books, with a fourth wall of beveled glass windows looking out to the seemingly endless pastures. This was one view that progress hadn't disturbed. Red was seated in a brown leather club chair by the fireplace, a few small logs ceremoniously lit for mood. His hand held a cut glass highball, with two fingers of a caramel brown spirit. Bourbon, I assumed.

Luke peeked his head into the room. "Father?"

"Luke, come on in," said Red, standing. "How are you, son?" He extended his hand. Not a hugger, I see. Good to know.

"I'm well, thank you," he said, taking his dad's hand. "Father, I'd like you to meet Derek Walter." So formal. This was old school, and I knew better than to diverge from the script.

"Mr. Walcott, it's a pleasure, sir," I said, putting on my best smile and firmly shaking his hand.

"Please, call me Red, son," he said. "Luke knows I am fond of formalities, but I am learning to give a little, as I get older. Please, have a seat, won't you?"

Luke took the chair next to his dad and I sat opposite, a small carved mahogany table between us.

"Can I offer you gentleman a drink? Luke, I am sure you remember where the bar is. You snuck into it enough as a teenager." Stately, but with a sense of humor, Red was slowly starting to grow on me.

Luke went over to the liquor cabinet and poured two bourbons, neat.

"Now, Derek, you are Barry Henry's nephew, isn't that right?" I nodded, consciously keeping my words to a minimum. "Barry is a good man. We have been close friends for years. He thinks quite highly of you."

"He has very kind words for you, as well, sir." Careful, Derek. Two sips of liquor and I was already testing my boundaries. Red showed no reaction. The perfect negotiating face. I had not broken my promise to Barry and I had never disclosed Red's youthful dalliances with my uncle to Luke. That was their secret, not mine. But I knew to hold that card close to my chest, for safekeeping.

Red moved the conversation forward, wisely. He and Luke covered the weather and sports and a few local land deals that he was negotiating, but so far we avoided the giant elephant in the room. Perhaps we should say elephants, at this point. We were approaching circus proportions, after all. The feud with Lana, the CCCP, the attention placed on the family, his son's sexuality, even the simple fact that I was sitting by Luke's side as his boyfriend, and not just another dinner guest.

The doorbell rang again and jarred me from my reverie. I took another calming sip of bourbon. Careful, Derek.

"That must be your sister," said Red. "Shall we move on to the parlor?" So the library was for the men, but the parlor was for entertaining the ladies, I assumed? He rose, leaving his empty glass behind, and left the room

"So far, so good," whispered Luke as we followed.

"Really? We haven't said much of anything."

"Business and family decisions are preceded by lots of small talk and pre-dinner drinks," he said. "This is what my father would refer to as foreplay, if he'd ever say the word. Nothing is abrupt. 'Small steps lead the way to victory,' he'd tell us as kids."

We entered the foyer just in time to see Rosa and Lana talking. Rosa was less animated with Luke's sister, not nearly as open as I had seen her with Luke. Lana was standing with her arms folded across her chest, smiling. I wouldn't say there was a chill between them. There was definitely a connection, but it was more servant/child than mother/ daughter. That changed the moment Red came into view.

"Daddy!" she cried, and threw open her arms. I bet when she was a kid she'd climb right up and demand to be carried to the next room. It was obvious, she was a daddy's girl, and he babied her every step of the way.

"How is my Lana Banana?" he said, his wide grin showing off every tooth in his mouth. Why Red, you old softy. You do have a heart. Formal and scholarly with Luke, Red was more at ease with Lana. I was beginning to understand these family dynamics.

Small talk and greetings were made all around. Of course, Lana and I had already met. She wasn't cold, but she wasn't warm and fuzzy, either. She was keeping up appearances, and I was happy to play along. I'd take what I could get. Small steps lead the way to victory, right Red?

Rosa led us into the parlor, where a majestic oil paint-ing of Posy Walcott hung over the fireplace, surveying the entire room, her straight blond hair smoothed back into a bun, diamonds in her ears and a tiered diamond necklace around her throat, her thin hands placed firmly on either side of her Queen Anne chair. She commanded attention in her pale blue gown. Another liquor cabinet stood ready for us to pillage. I remembered Luke's words of caution and made a mental note to sip the next one slowly. I'm sure the foreplay was about to give way to an intense discussion, and I had a feeling I would need my mind to remain clear.

Two cocktails in and sure enough, Red took charge and addressed his progeny.

"Lana, sweetheart. Luke. I want this nonsense to stop, you hear me?" Boom, right to the heart of the matter. It was less of a question and more of an order.

"Daddy," Lana smiled, sweetly, "perhaps we should discuss this, just the three of us? It is, after all, a family matter." As if she was saving Rosa and me the trouble and we should be grateful. I was about two seconds from taking her up on that offer, when I felt Luke's hand land itself firmly on my knee. I wasn't going anywhere.

"Lana, darling, everyone in this room is family, as far as I am concerned." Red spoke with such gravitas and firmness. I was enthralled, hanging on every word. Were these the fireworks I was waiting for all evening? This was about to get good!

Lana settled demurely into her seat, sizing up the room. She knew that Red had the floor, and she respected that.

"Lana, you have made your point. Publicly," Red began, the last word dripping slowly from his mouth. "You have made it clear that you do not approve of your brother's choices."

"Daddy, it's not…"

"Lana!" Red cut her off, immediately. Here it comes, I thought. "Lifestyle." "Choices." Would we ever reach a point in our civilization where this was no longer a discussion? Had I spent too many years in the liberal stronghold of New York City? Honestly, the only choice I made was to come back and deal with these outdated arguments in the South. I took a healthy sip of bourbon and kept my mouth shut, wisely.

"Your brother is a homosexual." Oh, shit. He went there! "You may not approve, but you must love him, and

I know you do. The world has changed, Lana. Not always for the best, but a smart businessman either has to adapt, or die. Now in my day, we did not discuss these things in open rooms. Of course we knew homosexuals. I had friends who were homosexuals. I still do. But anything discussed in the bedroom or the bathroom was not a proper topic for the parlor. It just was not gentlemanly, or ladylike. You may recall a Cole Porter song called "Anything Goes," but I imagine even he would be shocked by the carefree discussions in which we now find ourselves. Regardless, we stand here tonight having that very discussion. I have met your brother's companion, and I can tell you all that I approve. He comes from a good family, he is well mannered, and your brother has chosen him. That is good enough for me."

Luke's hand was a vice grip on my knee. This is the moment, I said to myself. This is the moment I must remember to tell our kids. Wait. Did I need to reconsider my views on a family of our own, after all? Hold that thought for another time, Derek. Right now, my heart was no longer beating. It felt like it had stopped, and I was hanging on every word that Red said.

"As for you, Lana, I hope that you one day find the right companion with whom to share your life." Whoa! Did he just jump over the gender there, in deference to Luke? This was indeed a monumental night. Who needs to get sloshed to have fun? This was amazing!

He paused. Here it comes. "As you all know, I have found such a companion in Rosa."

Rosa beamed, a woman in love. Had he ever acknowledged her in such a way, before? I had to ask Luke later, because there was no way I was getting off this roller coaster right now.

"Daddy," Lana was defiant. "Rosa is not my mother, and she never will be."

This evening was about so much more than Luke and me, and I was just beginning to realize it. How selfish of me. How self-centered I had been. All families have moments of realignment. The power dynamics shift and adjust. New teams are formed. Pacts are broken and re-written, more favorably for all, rather than for a single individual. Tonight wasn't about the argument between Lana and Luke; it was about the future of the Walcotts. I was just a witness, an attendee who had been magnanimously invited into the fold, and I was grateful.

"Lana, dear," Red said, "you are correct. Rosa is not your biological mother; however, she raised you and your brother and spent far more time with you than your mother ever deigned, before her untimely and unfortunate passing. I will not speak ill of the dead. I have never said a single disparaging word about your mother. But you must know, Lana, your mother was not a kind woman. Your memories of her are derived from fading photographs and press clippings. She was severe in her words and actions, more so than you probably remember. I loved her dearly. I did. But the marriage I had with your mother was decidedly transactional, and the love I feel for Rosa is more grounded in warmth and respect. If I am today to tell you to respect the love that Rosa and I share, than I would be circumspect to allow you to continue to disregard the love your brother so obviously feels for Derek."

The room fell silent. What could we possibly say after that eloquent speech? The only choice was to accept Red's demands. He was clearly in charge.

Lana spoke up, quietly. "I'm not sure I can stop it all, Daddy. It got out of hand. Amber, the CCCP, the protesters. Maybe it's bigger than me, now?"

"That is not the attitude of a Walcott," said Red, firmly. Discussion over. "You will do your best. I will not have the family name paraded through the news reports for the wrong reasons, anymore."

Lana deflated. "Yes, Daddy. I'll do my best." And that was that. She agreed to try and calm down the CCCP and get them to back off. Of course I was thrilled, but we weren't out of the water yet. No telling if she could calm the dogs of war that she had spent so many weeks whipping into a frenzy.

The doorbell rang, and Rosa practically jumped out of her seat. Red sat unmoving, and Lana looked over to Luke and me as if to say *who's that?*

"If you'll excuse me," said Rosa, and she walked out of the room, partially closing the doors to the parlor behind her. Red walked over to the liquor cabinet and topped off his bourbon, then stood waiting at the fireplace, the gentleman of the manor, one hand on the mantle. What was going on?

The front door opened and we heard Rosa say warmly, "Welcome to our home," just as she had said to Luke and me.

"Daddy? Are we expecting visitors?" asked Lana.

Red ignored her, choosing instead to take a sip of bourbon. If it was good enough for Red, it was good enough for me. I took a fortifying gulp.

We heard a voice in the hall. A woman. "I'm confused. What are we doing here?" she said.

Wait. What?! I know that voice...

15

THE FIRST SUPPER

Was I hearing things? I had to be.

I turned to Luke to see if he shared my reaction, but he remained stoic, staring straight forward. This had been quite an evening, so far. My internal dialogue was practically screaming to be set free, but I knew better than to release it here. That had to wait.

The doors to the parlor were pulled back, and there was Rosa, with a couple standing by her side.

"Bammy?" I practically sputtered. I couldn't help it. I couldn't be silent any longer. No one even looked at me, though. All eyes in the room, including Posy's, were focused on Bammy and her boyfriend.

"Michael, what is going on here? Will someone please tell me what is going on?" asked Bammy, quietly.

Red walked over to them from his position by the fireplace and extended his hand. "Miss Talbot, it is a pleasure to meet you. I am Red Walcott. Please, call me Red. May I call you Bammy?"

"Um, yes," she stammered, "certainly. But still, I have no idea why we are here."

"I will be happy to explain everything," said Red. "Please, take a seat." He directed them to the love seat across from the couch where Luke and I were sitting. Lana was seated in a chair to their left. Bammy and I exchanged puzzled glances, but Red had made it clear that he was in charge tonight. We were just participants.

"Would either of you care for a drink?" he asked, the perfect host.

"No, sir," replied Michael. "I think we should proceed without, if you don't mind. Perhaps we'll need one after?"

Perhaps? Hell, I needed a refill already. So much for me trying to take it easy. Lana's back was ramrod straight, her hands gripping the arms of her chair. She was ready to pounce. Lana wasn't the type who responded well to changes of plan, and this evening was certainly throwing her off her game. Luke shifted to the edge of the couch. He had barely touched his drink. I couldn't read his mind, but I imagine he was just as confused as the rest of us.

Bammy, ever the problem solver, spoke up first. "Sir, may I ask, am I invited here tonight in my capacity as principal? Because I can assure you, I am doing everything in my power to diffuse this difficult situation. The school doesn't like the extra attention, and I can imagine you and your family don't, either. Luke and Derek are fantastic educators, and I'm working to…"

"Bammy, please," Red held up his hand to stop her. "I have no doubts you are doing exactly as you describe, and I thank you for that. I am appreciative of your efforts. However, that is not the main reason for our

gathering tonight, though it may have been the impetus."
He paused and scanned the faces in the room, all paying
rapt attention to the gentleman standing at the fireplace.
"I have asked you all here," he began, "to correct a dis-
service. And to do so, I must start at the beginning. Lana
dear, I apologize in advance, as you may find some of
this deeply upsetting. If we have learned anything from
the past few weeks, though, it is just how important family is, and how even more important it is that we remain
united when confronted with a challenge. As I expressed
earlier this evening, my late wife Posy was a very special
woman. I do not fault her, though. Quite the contrary.
We knew what we were getting into when our marriage
was agreed upon. I hesitate to say 'arranged,' although
it did have the perception of a business arrangement
between the Walcotts and the Lindberghs. A unity that
would truly bless me with two beautiful children, Luke
and Lana. Posy and I loved each other; indeed, there is
no question about that. However, after you were born,
Lana, Posy felt that her motherly duties had been ful-
filled. I accepted that, yet I did not realize that she also
assumed an immediate cessation to our intimacy in the
bedroom."

Lana blushed slightly, but she was hanging on every
word, as were the rest of us. If we were to get stuck on one
word or turn of phrase, we may miss the good part, and I
just knew there was a juicy part on its way.

"It is no secret to you all that I turned to Rosa for
companionship," he continued, and nodded her way.
"We were discreet, of course. It was not my intention to
embarrass your mother or this family. I assure you now,

we had no intention of divorcing, we still enjoyed each other's company, and we had built quite a satisfying life together. Your mother remarked privately that she was actually pleased that Rosa was there for me, as that freed her for her own pursuits, her charity meetings, and so forth. This was simply a different time, one that I do not expect you all will understand fully. This arrangement worked for us."

He took another sip of his bourbon, then set his glass down on the mantle.

"Rosa, would you join me here, please?" She walked over from the entrance to the parlor and stood by his side, her arm around his waist. They were an odd match, the land tycoon and the Mexican nanny, but the love they shared was obvious.

"Rosa, my love," he said. "I apologize to you with all my heart for taking so long to correct this. I do hope you will forgive me?"

"*Si, mi amor,*" she practically beamed.

He picked up his story. "Lana, soon after you were born, Rosa confirmed to me that she was pregnant, as well. Posy could handle my indiscretion, but she was not prepared to deal with her husband's mistress having a child, and I do not fault her for that. Rosa gave birth while on an extended vacation, and the decision was made to give the child up for adoption when she returned. We all agreed on this, all three of us, so if there is blame or anger to be had, we all deserve our share."

Lana was as pale as a ghost and Luke was slack jawed. Bammy's eyes were wide open, and she turned to look at Michael, his face as stoic as Luke's had been, earlier.

"Michael," said Red, "I do hope you forgive us our sins, as we truly felt we made the only decision we could, at the time. Welcome to the family, son."

Michael nodded, in acceptance, but didn't utter a word. This wasn't news to him, after all. He wasn't experiencing the shock of a lifetime. Oh, how I felt for Luke and Lana.

The silence that followed felt eternal, but it probably only lasted 15 seconds. Personally, I wanted to scream, to laugh, to jump up and down. I had a million questions, but I fought myself to remain silent. Eyes darted about the room. Lana to Luke. Luke to Rosa. Rosa to Michael. Michael to Bammy. Bammy to me.

"Michael." The name cut through the silence. You know when you haven't spoken in awhile, and your voice clears the cobwebs with the first breath? He cleared his throat, and tried again, stronger. "Michael. Welcome, brother." And with that, Luke walked over and embraced his new family member.

Bammy started crying. I'm not really sure why. Maybe all the pressure we've been under lately, combined with this latest bombshell, was just too much? Maybe she was upset that Mayor Bellman wasn't Michael's dad? I'm kidding. Lana looked shell-shocked. No tears, but she wasn't ready with words, yet. She stood up and walked over to Michael and gave him a hug, following her older brother's lead. Her arms were listless, yet she forced them to activate, and they found their way around her new half brother's torso.

From there, everything became blurry. We all huddled in corners, carrying on conversations both whispered and in the open, tears, laughter, moments of complete shock, acceptance, and wonder.

"Are you okay?" I asked Luke, as we had a moment to ourselves, the new, expanded family getting to know one another.

"Yeah, of course," he said. "I mean, I think I am. I'm kind of numb. Michael's a great guy, though, so that softens it. My new little half brother could have been a dick, right?" He laughed. I'm glad he was seeing the humor in this.

"This was the craziest family dinner ever," I said. "And dinner hasn't even started."

"I wonder how long they've been planning to tell us this?" he questioned, out loud.

"I don't know, but your family has just passed mine in drama. And my family has a secret drag queen and a father who deserted us. I would never in a million years believe you would have topped that."

"Trust me," he said. "It wasn't a competition I was looking to win."

Red was comforting Lana, trying to explain more details that she required to get through this. Bammy and Michael came over and joined us.

"So, Derek," said Michael, "I guess we're the new guys around here, huh?" he joked.

"Yep," I said. "There's a pretty strict set of rules and regulations, though. You'll get the manual with your membership card. You're a quick learner, right? Oh, and how do you feel about a country club membership?"

"Stop it," said Luke. "We're not that bad. I guess you've been talking to my father and Rosa for awhile, now?" he asked Michael.

"Yeah, I have," he said. "It's funny. I never would have requested the paperwork if this one hadn't pestered me."

He held Bammy tighter by the waist and gave her cheek a light stroke with his free hand. "Turns out Nancy Drew here thought Mayor Bellman was my biological father. That's what she gets for snooping."

Bammy looked embarrassed.

"So, obviously it wasn't Bellman," I nudged, wanting to know more.

"No, not at all," said Michael. "I was doing Internet searches on him because I was looking for a smoking gun, some sort of leverage we could use to stop these ridiculous protests. I was trying to help you guys out."

I had something that could help us, of course, but outing the mayor as a cross dresser was not something I was comfortable with.

"That makes total sense. See what happens when we assume, Bammy?" I said, teasing her.

"Yeah. You're an ass," she deadpanned, then looked to Michael. "Can I please start drinking now?"

■ ■ ■

Dinner went surprisingly well. Rosa had prepared an enormous Mexican feast, and everyone gorged as if it was their last supper, and not the first as an extended family. Red sat on one end of the long dining table, with Lana to his left and Michael seated to his right. Rosa took her place at the opposite end, with Luke by her side. Bammy and I exchanged *how the hell did we end up here?* glances throughout the meal, but somehow we survived.

Red was keen to get Michael involved in his business, and Bammy spoke highly of her boyfriend, calling him a "financial wizard." Michael said he wanted to continue working with the school board, to remain close to Bammy, but he'd be happy to make room for additional work with Red. The two of them were off to a fine start.

At one point in the evening I overheard a whispered conversation between Lana and Red, meant to stay between the two of them, I supposed. "This won't affect my inheritance, will it Daddy?" Oh, Lana, always looking out for number one. Red assured her that Michael was only interested in getting to know them, and he laid no claim to any inheritance, though I doubted that Red would leave this Earth without making sure one of his children was financially supported.

Luke was quiet, but smiling. He preferred to be along for the ride, rather than make himself the center of attention. Perhaps that's why we balanced each other out so well? He laughed along with Rosa and asked Michael questions to get to know him better, now as a brother, and not just a friend. The stress of the last few weeks had really begun to show on his face, so I was grateful that he was enjoying himself. He was such a strong, supportive man, always worrying about others, but rarely noticing when he, himself, needed a break. I was happy to see him just relax, for a change.

The meal came to a natural close, and Red called us to attention, once more, asking for a toast. We raised our glasses to welcome Michael into the family, and he forcefully reminded Lana and Luke that their public turmoil must be resolved, as soon as possible. We knew that we had a week before the public school board meeting, so it was up to the three of us to work together to figure this out.

We began to stand up, one by one, reaching for dishes to help carry them to the kitchen.

"No, no, no!" said Rosa. "Leave it, leave it! I'll take care of it later." I don't know how she did it all by herself. Luke explained to me later that there was indeed a small household staff, but that they only worked daytime shifts. Red preferred his privacy at night. Old habits, I guess.

Coats were fetched and we all began kissing our good-byes and shaking hands. I was suddenly aware of how welcome I felt at the end of the evening, considering how nervous I was when I arrived. Red and Rosa both made me feel comfortable, and I was incredibly appreciative. I needed to work on Lana a bit, but I was hopeful that our relationship would change, in time. I tend to grow on people. At least I like to think I do.

"Oh, *mijo*!" said Rosa to Luke. "I forgot your tamales. I'll be right back," and she went into the house, leaving me, Lana and Luke standing outside. Bammy and Michael had already left and Red was safely ensconced within his fortress, again.

"So," said Luke.

"So," Lana replied.

"Seriously?" I said, flabbergasted. "Your father is the most verbose man I have ever met. After a roller coaster of a night like that, all you two have to say to each other is 'So?' Unbelievable!"

"I think we take after our mama that way," said Lana, softly. "You never met her, of course, so you wouldn't know. Daddy uses words to take over a room. Mama just needed one good look."

"I thought about Mother a lot tonight, Lana," said Luke, taking his sister's hands. "She would have been proud of us, for accepting Michael, for picking up the pieces and just moving on. Mother wasn't one for dramatics. If she were still here, she would have never allowed us to get this far in a fight. So... let's shut this thing down, okay? We need to talk strategy."

"Well, we have to start with Amber," said Lana. "I'll arrange a lunch with her tomorrow and see what needs to happen to bring this to a close."

"I don't get it, Lana," he said. "All these years, Amber has followed you around like a puppy dog. She worships you. Won't she do anything you tell her to do?"

"Luke, I can't get into it right now. Trust me. Amber is the key to this whole thing."

"What are you not telling me, Lana?"

"Big brother, you were always so good at sports. How the hell did you end up sucking so badly at math?"

"*Tamales!* Here you go!" Rosa appeared at the door and handed a paper bag to each of the siblings. "Heat those in the oven with just a touch of water in the pan. The microwave will dry them out." Kisses, then she left to rejoin Red.

Lana walked towards her car. "I'll give you a ring tomorrow and tell you what happens."

"Okay," he called out to her. "But, I.... Good night?" Math?

16

CAN I HAVE A PONY?

We couldn't expend any more energy worrying about Lana's riddle. We were exhausted, emotionally and physically, and we just needed to get to bed as soon as possible.

We barely spoke. What more was there to say? It had been one hell of an evening.

I started laughing to myself, quietly, as Luke pulled the car into his driveway, the porch light welcoming us home.

"What's so funny?" he asked, turning off the ignition.

"Oh, nothing important," I said, dreamily. "I was just imagining what it would be like if Michael and I appeared on Oprah together. 'And *you* get a dad! And *you* get a dad!' Awesome, right?"

"You're crazy, you know that?"

"Yeah, kinda. But you like me."

"That I do," he said, reaching out to place his hand reassuringly on my knee. "That I do."

■ ■ ■

I woke up Saturday morning to a flurry of text messages from Bammy. Apparently Michael had put on a brave face last night, but when they got home, he released the barriers, and the tears flowed. He had told his foster parents about the Walcotts long before he contacted Red and Rosa, and they supported him 100% in whatever he decided to do. They loved him like their own son, and he felt the same. He would never change his last name, but these immense feelings of guilt overcame him. Bammy experienced a long night of hand holding and reassuring hugs. I understood. We both had been thrust upon the Walcotts, with different degrees of expectations. I knew Luke would be the best person to help him through this.

"Babe?" I called out to him in the shower. "What are your plans today?"

"I'm hanging out here," he answered. "I need to be ready when Lana calls. No telling what she and Amber are up to."

"All right, I'm heading to Mom's. She wants me to help her clear some downed branches and underbrush from the yard. I'll call you later? Oh," I added, "do me a favor? Bammy messaged me. Michael had kind of a rough night. Can you make sure to reach out to him today? Maybe you two can meet up for a brotherly beer, or something?"

"Good idea. Will do!"

I drove Willie Nelson over to Mom's and walked inside. I didn't have to ring the doorbell at this house. Uncle Barry was sitting at the breakfast table in his kimono, having a plate of sliced carrots and hummus. Since his coming out we'd all agreed to stop calling it a dressing gown.

"How's the diet going? I asked.

"How do you think?" he growled back at me. "I may just be too old to change, you know that? My body is quite happy where she is. Maybe I should just listen to her. Besides, a bigger backside just means more sparkles on my dress." He laughed, as if he was just getting used to the idea of liking himself, no matter what. His public performance as Beret had been good for him.

"Is there anything good to eat?" I asked. "I haven't had breakfast yet."

"Only healthy things," he said, grumpily. "Audrey's been on a health food kick."

"Really? She loves fried foods. I was hoping for biscuits and gravy."

"I can still make you biscuits," she said, entering the kitchen from her bedroom. She was tying the knot on her bathrobe, a glowing smile on her face. "But we don't have any pork sausage. Johnny says it's not good for you, how they make it. I have some of that veggie sausage, if you want?"

"Veggie sausage? That's sacrilege, Mom! What's next? Barbecued tofu?"

"Oh, hush," she said. "It's not that bad."

"Not bad at all," said Johnny, following her through the door, his shoes in his hands.

Wow. So we're at that stage, now? "Walk of shame, Johnny?" I teased.

"Nothing shameful about it. She's still my wife, after all." So that answered that question. They never did sign those papers. Interesting.

Johnny gave my mom a kiss that was befitting a couple far younger than their years, then he clasped my shoulder, nodded at Barry and walked out the side door, without a word.

I yelled after him. "Can I have a pony?" I glanced over at Barry, thinking he'd enjoy the joke. He did not look happy.

"Do you want me to make you something?" she asked.

"No, I'm fine. I'll have some cereal. We still have milk, right?"

"Is soy okay?"

■ ■ ■

After I helped her clear the yard, Mom went back inside to clean up and I took a seat in the old rocking chair on the front porch, surveying the lawn. The house was surrounded by trees, with a long gravel driveway that led to an old country road. It was quiet out here. Peaceful. I heard the screen door open behind me and Barry came out with two glasses in his hand.

"I figured you could use a cocktail after all that work," he said, handing me a cool drink.

"Thanks." I glanced at him as he took a seat beside me. "So, dare I ask? Is he hanging out a lot, now?"

"What did she say?"

"I didn't bring it up," I said, sipping my drink. Vodka and sweet tea. That hit the spot. "She tends to be a little secretive, you know?"

"Aren't we all?" he said. "Family trait."

"I take it you're not pleased?"

He sighed, rocking slowly. "I need to lighten up a little, I guess. I was kind of hard on him, at the beginning. When he left, you two had nothing. No safety net. It was up to Janey and me to help out, and we were glad to do it, of course, but it feels a little strange for me to just forgive and forget, after all these years. He does seem like he's changed a lot, for the better." He paused, then spoke adamantly. "*We* raised you, kid. *We* did. Not him. And I'm damn proud of the man you've become. I'm just feeling a little conflicted. He waltzes in, years later, as suave as he always was, and now you're all just perfect and waiting for him. We did all the work and he's sharing in the reward."

"It's not like that," I assured him. "I'm not ready to trust him 100%, either. But in a way, you're right about one thing. It *is* years later. We're all adults now. We can make our own decisions, and that includes Mom, too. You don't need to protect us all, anymore, okay?"

"How'd you end up being so smart?" He shook his head.

"Good teachers, I guess. But my favorite one was the lady in the sparkly dress."

"Go ahead. Make me cry," he said, defiantly. "I've been dying to know if this waterproof mascara really works. If not, I'm returning it."

■ ■ ■

I called Luke as I was leaving, but he didn't answer the phone. Maybe he was out having a beer with Michael, like I suggested?

"Luke? You here?" I called out as I opened the door, but there was no answer. His car was in the driveway and his keys were here. Maybe he went for a walk? Or Michael picked him up?

I walked back into the kitchen and set my bags down on the counter. After leaving Mom's I was in the mood to reaffirm my lifelong status as a carnivore, so I bought some barbecue from Cochon's on the way over. I looked out on the back porch, and there was Luke sitting alone. I pushed open the screen door and peeked my head out.

"Hey, what's up?" I asked. "I picked up barbeque. I didn't think we'd feel like cooking tonight."

He didn't answer. He was sitting in his deck chair, staring out silently into the woods, empty beer bottles at his feet and covering the table in front of him.

"Babe? Did you hear me?" I walked closer to him and the door closed itself behind me. "Are you drunk? Did you and Michael have your own little beer fest out here or something?"

He took a final swig from the bottle in his hand, emptied it, and reached for another from the table.

"Babe… you're scaring me. Are you okay? Talk to me." I pulled up a chair and sat facing him, breaking his sightline to the trees. He looked so sad. What happened?

"I met Amber today." His voice was soft, yet broken, as if he had been wounded. "Remember what you said about you and Michael being on Oprah?"

"Yeah, I do, but…"

"Well, you may as well invite Jett along to the taping. He got a new dad today, too."

"No." It sounded like a whisper coming from my lips, as if someone else was speaking for me.

"Yep. Me. I'm Jett's father."

■ ■ ■

I walked him inside the house and set him down on the couch, wrapping a blanket around his shoulders and handing him a glass of water. I started the coffee pot and gathered up the bottles on the back deck, putting them in the recycling bin by the door. He takes care of me all the time. Always. It was my turn to step up.

"Luke, we have food if you want some, but there's no rush."

"I don't feel like eating. Did you get pulled pork?"

"Yes. And hushpuppies and green beans."

"Okay. I feel like eating." Well, that was a good sign. At least he wasn't in the mood to torture himself. I made two plates of food and brought them into the living room, setting them down on the coffee table in front of us.

"Do you want to talk? Or just eat? No pressure. You decide."

"I just feel kind of numb. I don't know what to say." He took a bite of his sandwich, but he looked a bit like a zombie eating a body, not caring where the chunks of flesh fell. I reached up with my napkin and wiped his face. He was really not himself.

Two cups of coffee and a full meal later, we were still on the couch, and he was feeling a little better.

"Thanks for taking care of me," he said. "Sorry I was such a mess when you got here."

"No worries at all, babe."

"I went over to Amber's today. Lana called me and asked me to meet them there."

"And?"

"Lana knew. All these years. She knew Jett was my kid."

"Holy shit. But are you sure? I mean, I know that sounds awful of me, but should we get a paternity test?

"That's what Lana was saying. About the math. It makes sense. That's why she was always trying to get me and Amber back together."

"Let me guess? I messed that up for good?"

He looked over to me, his eyes so troubled. "Not you. Us. We did that, together."

"So, this whole thing… it was 'kind of' about us being gay, but mostly just about Amber feeling rejected and wanting revenge, and Lana wanting you to get back together with her best friend? And they did all of this?" I was floored.

"What's that quote about a 'woman scorned?' Yeah. They went pretty far."

"Damn," I said, quietly. "I have to give Amber mad props for her follow through. When she sets her sights on a plan, she goes for it. Three husbands later, even. Talk about playing a 'long game.' So, what do we do now? Is it over?"

"I don't know." He sounded defeated. "That's just it. We didn't agree on a solution. She wants time to think. She wants me to meet with Jett, of course. She still wants me back, Derek, and I don't think she'll accept anything less. It's crazy. The kids go back to school on Monday, but you and I are still suspended through the week, no matter what. Then we have the school board meeting on Friday."

"And who knows what will happen then?" I asked.

"Exactly."

"Well," I said, firmly, "it's super important that those kids don't go back to school. Not until this is over. It's still about the money. I've got calls to make. You just relax. I've got this."

■ ■ ■

Since I didn't have to work on Monday, I agreed to meet Johnny for lunch at his parents' old place. It was kind of nice to be free, but honestly, I would have rather been at the school. I actually liked teaching, and I felt like I was having a positive effect on the kids' lives, just as so many teachers had influenced mine.

I was walking out the door to run some errands before meeting my dad, when I received a text from Bammy. "No kids," was all it said. I gave her a quick call.

"Does this message mean what I think it does?" I asked.

"No one showed up. Only a handful of kids. Like they didn't get the secret memo," she whispered. "We had to send teachers home. We've consolidated classes and we're basically conducting an eight hour study hall. The school board is freaking out."

"Amazing," I said, smiling. "Let's see if they can make it till Friday. Operation Walkout continues. I'll catch you later."

I didn't tell her about Jett. I didn't tell anyone. It wasn't my place. I promised Luke that until he dealt with it privately, I wouldn't discuss it publicly, though I strongly suggested to him that he share the news with Michael. They both had dealt with shocking news in the last week, and they could support each other, I figured. That's what brothers are for, right? Suddenly, I was carrying a huge suitcase of secrets. Jett, Belle, Miss Mabel, Red and Barry. It was almost too much for a talker like me.

I drove over to Pleasant Hills, the subdivision that Red had put together in the deal when he sold Johnny's family farm. There was nothing pleasant about it. Road after road of McMansions, one piled on top of another, with absolutely no privacy. And hills? Were they kidding? It used to be a farm. All the hills had been plowed down years ago. Only the trees by the main road were large. The rest were newly planted saplings, waiting their turn.

Thankfully, Johnny was smart enough to save a few acres around the original farmhouse, so it still felt like he was a bit removed from the creeping civilization. I preferred it that way.

The house was dusty and fairly unorganized, objects scattered here and there. It looked like Johnny had been excavating boxes, unearthing memories from his youth.

"I like what you've done with the place," I teased.

"It could use a woman's touch, for sure," he said.

"Speaking of…"

"Is that why you wanted to meet me? To put the hammer down on me and your mom?"

"No, not at all," I said. "But I do want to get a better idea of what you're thinking. Do you mind sharing?" If I learned anything from that night at the Walcott's, it was that getting to the point quickly was the way to get things done.

We took a seat at the old table in the kitchen. It was one of those 1950s Formica dinette sets, with teal and white stripes. Amazing. Kit would love it.

"Did Barry send you?" he asked. "He doesn't trust me yet. I don't blame him." He reached for the teapot and poured us two cups.

"How's your reentry?" I asked, figuring I'd start from a simpler place. "Coming back to Parkville isn't easy. I know."

"The town's changed a lot. But then again, it hasn't. Same families. Updated issues. It's still home." He handed me a cup.

"You plan on sticking around?"

"I'm not running away this time, Derek. I promise."

"I'll hold you to that," I said, sipping my tea. "But you've gotta make up with Barry. He should be first on your list, right now."

"Any suggestions would be most appreciated," he said, his hands wrapped around the mug in front of him.

"Well, he's really fond of diamonds."

17

NO MORE SECRETS

Tuesday morning arrived and even fewer kids showed up at the school than the day before. It seemed the word was officially out. Bammy called to tell me that they decided to send everyone home, including the teachers. The school board was extremely anxious to resolve the situation, and they were simply counting the days until the public meeting on Friday. They needed the kids in their seats in order to make their numbers, but the students weren't following the board's plan, they were following ours. And it was perfect.

I pulled Willie into Luke's street and immediately saw the shiny red Corvette parked in the road out front. Shit. Jett was here. I wondered if Luke was okay, but I didn't know if I should I leave them alone or get involved. I knew I was going to have to deal with this eventually, so I decided to throw my hat into the ring. Solidarity, right?

I opened the door, and the living room was empty. I stepped into the kitchen and could see Jett and Luke out on the back deck. Neither of them appeared to be physically wounded, so that was a good start. Nobody was bleeding. Jett was lounging casually in one of the deck chairs, legs wide open, one arm tossed languidly over the back of the chair. He didn't seem to have a care in the world, and the smirk on his face spoke volumes. Luke was sitting close by, hunched forward, elbows resting on his knees. His hands were clenched together and his brow was furrowed. It was plain to see who was in control of the situation, and I didn't like it.

"Hey there, Derek," Jett said, turning to face me as I opened the door to the porch. "Or should I call you 'step daddy' now? Pops and I haven't gotten that far, yet." Luke looked at me uncomfortably. Jett was enjoying every minute of this.

"Why don't we stick with 'Mr. Derek' for the time being?" I said, firmly. In the South, it's quite common for kids to call their elders by their first name, but as a sign of respect we add Mr. or Miss before it. I wasn't ready to welcome Jett with open arms just yet, even if he was Luke's son.

"All right then, *Mr. Derek*," he said pointedly, that self-satisfied grin still plastered on his face. "Pops and I were just talkin' visitation rights. Mom's place is totally better, but I'm sure I could have some pretty wicked parties back here, don't ya think? This deck is perfect for a kegger. Pops is gonna set up that second room for me to stay over and I'll be all set. Isn't that great?"

I looked at Luke to gauge his reaction. Jett is moving in? What the *hell*?

"Luke, could I borrow you for a minute, inside?" I said, with a bit too much edge in my voice. "I'm just about to head on over to Mom's house and I just wanted to show you that broken light that's acting funny. You mind?"

"Huh? Uh, yeah. Sure," he said. "I'll be right back, Jett."

"No sweat, Pops," and he threw his legs up over on the seat of the next chair, arms folded behind his head. "I'm not going anywhere."

Like hell you aren't, kid.

The door closed behind us and I pulled Luke into the hallway by the hand.

"Listen," he started, "before you say anything, he's my son, all right? Just cut me some slack. I have no clue what I'm doing here."

"Yeah," I nodded, eyes wide open, "that's kinda obvious. That kid's running all over you and loving every minute of it."

Luke put his hand to his forehead and sighed. "I don't know what to do, Derek. I'm his father, but I'm not. Everything is so fucked up right now. He just showed up on my doorstep. I told Amber that he and I should meet, but we didn't talk about when or where. I thought we would ease into this, slowly. But he's been here like an hour, and he's all 'Pops' this and 'Pops' that. He's pushing me, I know he is, but honestly, Derek, I'm kinda freaking out. I know I need to take responsibility, but I don't know how to be a parent, yet."

"It's okay, babe," I reassured him. "I can't even imagine what you're dealing with. Sorry. I'm sorry. I'll back off. You two need to get to know each other, for sure. But a keg party on the back porch isn't the way to do that. That kid's not dumb. He knows he can wrap you around his finger right now."

"Yeah, that's for sure," he admitted. "Whenever he starts talking, which is always, by the way, I just kind of freeze. My father wasn't the warm and fuzzy type, so I'm at a bit of a loss here."

"We'll figure it out together, right?" I said, my hand on his shoulder. "But first, your priority has to be Amber. And if Jett is the way to get her to stop the CCCP, then that's what we have to do."

"Jett said she wants me to come over for dinner tomorrow night," he said. "What should I do?"

"I think you should go. You have to."

"You're coming with, right?" he asked. "Please?"

"Babe, I think this is one you may have to take on your own. Amber won't take too kindly to me being there, especially if she's really in this for the reasons we think she is. We were supposed to meet Bammy and Michael tomorrow, but I'll send your regrets. I'm sure they'll understand."

"All right," he said, accepting his fate. "I'm going back out there. Wish me luck. I have to figure out a way to connect with my son."

"Good luck, *Pops*," and I gave him a friendly punch on the shoulder.

■ ■ ■

I met Bammy and Michael on Wednesday at the Tater Tot for dinner. They were already seated in a booth towards the back when I arrived.

"Hey," she said, getting up to give me a kiss, "I hope you don't mind, but we took a booth back here in the shadows. There are just so many whisperers, lately. I was hoping to be a little inconspicuous."

"Embarrassed to be seen with the enemy?" I teased as I took my seat.

"Derek, come on." She sounded tired. "I know you're joking, but I'm just at my wits' end, these days."

"I'm sorry, Bammy. I know. Let's get some cocktails and get to work."

The waitress came by and we ordered a round of drinks and appetizers. Bammy had called me the day before to suggest we meet to synchronize our next steps, even though they weren't 100% clear. There were a lot of *what ifs* and *maybes* coming up, but we had to be prepared for every situation, even when new monkey wrenches like Jett kept popping up.

"Luke sends his regrets," I said. "He's having dinner with Amber and Jett tonight."

"How's he dealing with the whole Jett situation?" asked Michael. "A new brother and a new son in one week can't be that easy."

"I'm so glad he talked about it to you," I said. "He felt a little better, after. He's dealing. It's tough. Not the brother part, of course, you're awesome. But Jett? He's a handful."

"I can imagine. At least I had some advanced notice," Michael said. "Thanks to my sneaky super spy girlfriend here." He put his arm around her and she just smiled. It was good to see that he wasn't holding her snooping against her.

"Well, Lana said that Amber was the key, and we're still counting on that," I explained. "If Luke can get her to call off the CCCP, then all of this will be over. I'm just worried about what he'll have to do to get her to agree to that."

"And if Amber doesn't budge?" asked Bammy.

"Then the school board will," said Michael. "And I'm afraid it probably won't be a result that you'll like. I've crunched the numbers, and the school is losing a ton of money on this fight, plus they are racking up negative publicity like nobody's business. Neither one is good. It's become a nuisance, and they see only one way out. If those kids don't get back on track on Monday, then you and Luke will most likely be out of a job."

"So, Luke and I are really losing our jobs over a kiss?" I said, the reality slowly setting in.

It was almost time to concede this one. But not quite yet. Come on, Luke. Work your magic charm on Amber.

■ ■ ■

He was sitting on the couch and nursing a beer when I got back home, watching some sports recap show on the television.

"How are Bammy and Michael?" he asked, as I kicked my shoes off and joined him, snuggling in.

"They're doing great." I reached for the remote and turned the volume down a bit. "We had a nice time. They've invited us over to dinner when this whole thing ends. How did it go with Amber?"

"You first." He wasn't smiling.

"Well," I frowned, "it doesn't look so good. According to Michael, if the CCCP doesn't go away and the kids aren't all back in school on Monday, then you and I are looking for new jobs."

He looked at me, defeated. "It's not much better on my end."

"What happened?"

"Amber pulled out all the stops tonight. She has this 'perfect family' fantasy, and that includes me and Jett. She was 'Suzy Homemaker' all night. Huge meal, dinner music, permanent grin on her face. We talked about our days as if we were one big happy family, avoiding any topic of real substance. It didn't take me long to realize that I'm supposed to play the part of the loving husband and Jett's role is the handsome, athletic son. It was a joke."

I could just picture Amber with her red hair in a bouffant, twirling around the kitchen in a red and white checked apron, happily waiting on her beautiful, imaginary family while cartoon bluebirds helped her tidy up. I shuddered.

"Jett went downstairs after dinner to play video games," Luke continued. "Amber asked me to join her on the couch for a drink. The stereo segued into a music playlist of all of our songs from high school. She actually dimmed the lights, Derek. She thought she was going to seduce me!"

"Seriously?! This is getting good!" I had to admire her brass.

"Stop," he winced. "It wasn't funny. I was freaking out, inside. I swear, she thought all she had to do was ply me with some drinks, play some old songs and let me get a good whiff of her perfume and I would just jump her bones. It was kind of sad, actually. I was polite, of course.

As polite as I could be, you know? But when I mentioned your name, she just went off. She started yelling at me, crying, telling me how I ruined her life, how I left her with a baby and she got stuck with three crappy husbands that she didn't want. She blames me for everything."

"Those were her choices, not yours, Luke," I reminded him. "She didn't even tell you she was pregnant, right?"

"No, of course not. If she had, I would have done the right thing. Or at least, I think I would have. This whole thing is a mess. I can't even get my brain around it. It's impossible to know what my nineteen-year-old self would have done, but it's too late to second-guess all that. Heck, I don't even know what I'm supposed to do *now*. Anyway, she flipped. It was pretty bad. She had this idea in her head that I would move in with them, that she would have the family she always wanted. I told her no, it's not gonna happen. I said I would be a part of Jett's life, of course, but that she and I were definitely not going to be a couple, again. Then the screaming really began. Jett came upstairs to watch her going off on me and he just stood there, leaning against the wall and laughing. It was too much. I can't give her what she wants. I walked out. I had to. It wasn't going anywhere good."

I reached down and held his hand. He looked exhausted, but I knew he had done his best. Given a choice between saving his job by being with Amber, or losing his job by being with me, he had chosen me. I felt terrible and great, all at once.

"Come on," I said. "Let's make some popcorn and crawl into bed and watch a movie."

"As long as it's not *The Parent Trap,* count me in," he said, smiling half-heartedly. He was keeping up a good face, but I knew this was tearing him up, inside.

■ ■ ■

Bammy called us Thursday afternoon to tell us that Mayor Bellman wanted to speak to us before the public hearing on Friday. So many people had expressed interest in attending that the school board decided to hold the meeting in the Parkville High gym, rather than in their offices, as they normally do. They had to make room for all of the reporters from the local and national stations.

We drove onto the school campus in Luke's car, and the crowds were enormous. The CCCP was out in full force, as well as our supporters from Love All. There were picket signs and huge banners and organized chants. The local police force was tasked with keeping both sides apart, as well as clearing an aisle in the center for us to make our way through.

Luke and I clasped hands and walked proudly towards the entrance with our heads held high. It's a strange thing, to feel like a criminal and a celebrity all at once. Both sides were so vociferous in their exclamations of condemnation and support that I could hardly wait for all of this to just be over. I like my share of attention, but this was out of control. The clamor was unbelievable. Hurry up and fire us, will you?

Bammy met us at the door and we took a moment to collect ourselves before quietly making our way into the school office. We had stopped for coffee on the way, of course, and I picked up an extra for Miss Mabel. It was just getting to be a habit, and I had felt bad that I hadn't seen her in a week. The office support staff had continued to work during the walkout, even though the students weren't attending. I placed the cup on her desk and she actually looked up at me today, for a change, and gave me a firm nod, without saying a word. I took this as a show of support, and it emboldened me. This was all worth it, right? No matter the end result? I had to believe that the answer was yes.

Bammy led us down the hall to her office, and Mayor Bellman was seated at his old desk. Grey hair, grey suit and grey skin, he didn't look very happy to see us. This was more of a nuisance than anything else, and he had an air about him that said *I've got better things to do than deal with this mess.*

"Derek, Luke, we appreciate y'all coming down here to talk with us before the meeting gets started," he began. "Y'all know Michael Taylor from the school board, and Principal Talbot, of course." Heads nodded around the room, but no one seemed to want to say anything. We all looked at each other with unsure faces, wondering what would happen next.

"Gentlemen," started Bellman, "I invited you here as a courtesy. Y'all know this just can't go on any longer. To be truthful, I couldn't give a rat's ass what y'all do at home. I've worked with both y'all and I think you've both done fine jobs here. But this isn't about that, and we all know it. The moment those kids walked out it all changed. We can handle a little disruption, of course, but I've discussed it with Michael here, and there's just no ifs, ands or buts about it. A school needs students to survive. And as long as y'all are here, no matter the reason, this walkout has continued and doesn't show any signs of letting up. We aren't left with many choices, unfortunately, so I wanted to give y'all a heads up before we head into that public meeting. But before I do, is there anything you'd like to say?"

Yes, there *is* something I'd like to say. I'd like to say that you're a hypocrite. You're a straight, married cross dresser who moonlights as a cabaret singer named Belle. You've been a member of the Bears' Club for years, and God only knows what kind of debauchery and "alternative lifestyles" and crazy moments you have witnessed in your lifetime, but you're a coward to let a kiss between two men ruin two promising careers and bring down an entire school because you won't stand up and let your voice be heard over the din of a few crazed zealots. I'm too good of a man to out you, Belle. I won't do that. But you're making it damn hard for me to stick with my decision. *That's* what I'd like to say.

"Yes," I started, then looked at Luke. We had made the decision the night before that we would resign, before they could fire us. "Luke and I are prepared to…"

"Y'all hold up one dang minute!" a voice exclaimed behind us.

We all turned our heads to see who had entered the room. It was Miss Mabel, and she was holding a student by the ear. It was Jett Winthrop?!

18

(DON'T) FIGHT THE POWER

"Let go of me, woman!" Jett screeched, in obvious pain. She may be small, but Miss Mabel appeared to have a death grip on that boy's ear.

"Don't you sass me, boy!" she replied, not letting go, the chain from her eyeglasses swinging as she shook her head. "I didn't drag you outta that gymnasium to give me no lip."

"What in tarnation is going on here, Miss Mabel?" Bellman bellowed as he stood up from the desk.

"This'll all be right as rain, shortly, Mr. Mayor," she said, "but right now, you're gonna sit down and listen to this boy. You hear me, *Belle?*"

Belle! *Holy shit!* That shut up Bellman but good. He threw her a look of pure shade, but sure enough, he sat his backside right down on that swivel chair in record time, his cheeks turning a bright crimson. Bless you, Miss Mabel!

She gave Jett's ear one final twist and pushed his body forward towards the mayor.

"*Ow!*" he yelped. "Miss Mabel, you've done lost your mind. Wait till my mom gets ahold of you!"

"I ain't afraid of your mama, Jett Winthrop," she said, "and you know that. Now you get up to that desk and you fix this mess. *Now!* Ya hear me?"

"I don't know what you're talkin' about," he said, and then looked to us for help. "She's gone crazy!" Poor, help-less Jett, my ass.

"*Don't you play no games with me, boy,*" she said. "My sis-ter done told me everything. You think she don't listen when she's scrubbin' your bathroom? Cleanin' up after you? Cookin' for you and your mama? Addie May done worked for Miss Amber long enough to collect her fair share of secrets. 'Bout time she shared some of them, dontcha think?" She stared at him, coldly, challenging him with her firm eyes. She meant business, and we all knew it. Whatever she had on him, it was good, and he knew he had lost.

He was so furious; he looked like he wanted to punch someone. Standing there with his fists clenched at his sides, cartoon steam coming out of his flaring nostrils, he surveyed his audience and realized he needed a change of course, and fast. Just as quickly as he had been angered, his mood switched instantly, and a snarled grin took over his face.

"I ain't doing this because of you, old lady," he sneered, spitting the words. "I already got what I want. This is *my* choice. You understand that?"

"Whatever helps you sleep at night, boy," she said. "Now are you gonna tell 'em? Or should I?" She glared at him fiercely, eyes narrowing.

Jett turned to face Luke. "Hey there, *Pops*," he taunted. "Hope you haven't renovated that extra room for me, yet. Looks like you're off the hook."

"What do you mean, Jett?" Luke said, slowly comprehending along with the rest of us.

"Wake *up*, man," he sneered. "Mom said you sucked at math, but seriously? *I'm not yours, okay?* You're not my dad. Never were."

Luke was clutching my hand, and he almost broke my fingers he squeezed so hard. My eyes grew wider, and I had to remind myself to breathe.

"*I'm not your father?*" he repeated, softly. "I'm not your father. I don't… but, *why?* Why did you *do* this?"

"Like I said, I got what I wanted already. How many teenagers do you know who drive brand new Corvettes? Mom wrote me a big fat check and all I had to do was figure a way to get you back into my house. She's been telling your sister that same old lie for years, keeping her in line. She figured it was time to spring it on you, too. And it would have worked if Miss Mabel hadn't butted in."

Nobody said a word. We were all speechless. Amber had bribed Jett to screw up Luke's life, in order to try and win him back?!

"Come on!" he laughed, hands up, playing to the crowd. "Y'all can't be angry at me, right? I'm just tryin' to make my mom happy. What's a good son like me supposed to do? Getting out of school for a week was just a bonus. Acting like we were all freaked out about these two," and he pointed at Luke and me. "Wake up, you old fossils! No one cares about that, anymore. We just didn't want to go to class, and y'all played right into it!"

Bellman couldn't take it, anymore. He rose from his desk in slow motion, eyeing Miss Mabel for approval.

She returned his nod, then she spoke up. "I trust y'all can handle this from here without me? I'll see y'all at the meeting. Good day," and with that, she closed the door behind her as she left the room.

"Jett Winthrop," said Mayor Bellman. "You are in for a world of trouble, son."

I had to cover my mouth with my hand. I was *this close* to laughing out loud.

■ ■ ■

Bellman and Jett came to an understanding quite quickly, though the sight of the mayor of Parkville negotiating terms with a sixteen year old student was quite ridiculous. There was no telling how far Bellman would go to keep his alter ego Belle covered up, but I guess this was proof of his intentions to keep that side of himself buried from the public. It seemed that no one in the room besides me had noticed Miss Mabel's intentional slip, and I made sure to keep my mouth shut.

Basically, Jett proudly admitted that he was messing with everyone's lives in order to make his mom happy. The way he saw it, his next moves only played out in his favor, as well. He viewed his change of tactic as a win, and that was fine by the mayor and the rest of us. Chip was Jett's best friend and a senior. He needed to graduate on time in order to start the summer football program at UT, and the school closure threatened to delay that, so Jett wanted to help him out. Also, by taking charge of the student body and basically telling them that it was cool to go back to class, he was setting himself up to be the self-appointed ruler of the school his senior year. Sure, his mom would be pissed off, but he didn't care about that, anymore. He got Luke to the house. It wasn't his fault that his mom couldn't seal the deal. Besides, he had his car, already. What was she going to do? Take it away? He was the only friend of hers that she hadn't lied to. She needed him. It was definitely an odd relationship.

Bammy and Michael quickly crafted three statements: one for the mayor, one for Jett and one for Luke and me. Together we walked over to the gymnasium, and Mayor Bellman spoke first. Cutting quickly to the chase, and hoping to avoid a nasty, public discussion, he started out by stating that all differences had been resolved. He explained his motives just as you imagine a politician would. He declared that although his personal views on same gender relationships had not changed, his larger, worldview had evolved, due to the ongoing public discussions that had been raised in the last week. There were boos, of course, but the mayor silenced them quickly, then ushered Jett onto the stage. Jett thanked the mayor and then went on to say he was speaking on behalf of the student body. He urged all students to return to classes on Monday, and thanked the CCCP for their efforts, but assured them that the students valued their education, and no further protests would be necessary. Again, more boos. Amber's face was bright red with anger. Jett would have a lot of explaining to do, later. Luke and I were up next, and the hecklers chimed in before we could even start. Mayor Bellman had to step up, again, to remind them to be civil, but we knew deep in our hearts that this fight wasn't really over. We may have won this battle, but this was just the beginning. We thanked our supporters and stated that we looked forward to a smooth return to our jobs and an end to the animosity of the previous weeks. We agreed, as the others did, that we now had a better understanding of the separation between our professional and private lives, and that the welfare of the students took precedence above all. In the end, *respect* was the key word oft repeated, but I liked to imagine that we now all agreed to *love all*.

■ ■ ■

Plenty of citizens made sure to have their moment at the public microphone, but the mayor kept the peace, and overall, the meeting was probably a bit of a let-down to our more vociferous opponents.

"Is it really over?" I asked Luke, as we stepped away from the podium after the mayor drew the events to a close.

"Yes and no. They may be kind to our faces, but they'll be talking about us behind our backs for a very long time," he said. "Southerners like a good public battle. And we never forget."

"In other words, we probably shouldn't order any wedding cakes any time soon, right?" I asked.

"I don't think so, babe," he said, putting his arm around me. "But seriously, I feel a huge weight lifted off my shoulders. Not only do we still have our jobs, but I was definitely not ready to be a father, yet."

"Well, I know what I *am* ready for," said Bammy, as she stood by us, smiling for the cameras. "Cocktails?"

The three of us made our way through the throng of reporters and gathered our friends and supporters along the way: Mom, Uncle Barry, Johnny, Kit, Shawn, Tommy, Meredith and Michael. Peaches and Tammy from Chesty Cheese were there, as well as Saul and Rachel. It felt like everyone we loved had come out to support us.

"Oh, honey, I'm so happy for you!" Mom said, giving me a kiss on the cheek.

"Congratulations, you two," said my dad. "You beat the system!" It was nice to hear some praise from my counter culture Zen dad.

"We are so *happy* for y'all!" said Meredith. "We have a whole case of champagne left over from the party. Drinks on us!"

"It only feels right to go back to where we started," I agreed. "Let's head to the gallery for a Love All celebration?"

"Day drinking!" yelled Kit, as if it were the best idea she had heard all day. We all headed to our cars. "See you there!"

We spotted Jett on the way out of the gymnasium. He was having a pretty intense discussion with Amber. She glared at us both as we passed, and Luke just nodded, solemnly. Their next conversation would have to wait. Now wasn't the time or the place. It seemed like these two would always have bad timing.

We walked as quickly as we could towards the parking lot. Luke unlocked the car door for me and I stepped inside, closing out the roar of the crowd surrounding us. I felt a bit like a celebrity who thought they would enjoy the attention, yet decided to flee the flashing bulbs, after all. Right now I just wanted to kiss my boyfriend. I still felt slightly "illegal," and I hoped that that feeling would pass soon. I had hated all of our sneaking around. It just wasn't my style, anymore, but being brazen certainly hadn't helped our standing in the community. We could definitely move forward as a couple, that was certain, but we needed to tread a little more lightly from here on out. Respect goes both ways, and we had learned that the hard way.

Luke and I didn't say much as we drove away from the school and onto the highway. We were both still in shock, I think. I looked over at him and smiled, and he did the same, but there was no doubt that all of the intensity of the last few weeks had exhausted us. My heart was still beating rapidly thinking about the last hour. We really just needed a good vacation after all of this.

"Ready to go inside and face our fans?" I said, as he parked the car on the street outside the gallery.

"With you, I can do anything," he said.

We entered that gallery to cheers and back slaps and lots of hugs and smiles. Champagne flutes were shoved into our hands and the room was filled with a raucous energy that increased as the night progressed. Later that evening, as the festivities were winding down, Luke excused himself to answer his phone. He wandered off to a corner, and held his fingers to his ear, blocking out the din of the celebratory music.

"Everything all right?" I asked, as he came back.

He reached for my hand again and held it firmly. "It was my father and Rosa," he said, smiling, "sending their congratulations." He looked relieved. "He's just as happy as we are that this is all over. We're expected for a family brunch on Sunday. I hope that's okay?"

"Sounds great," I said. "Do we need to…" My words trailed off, as I spotted Lana entering the gallery. That was a surprise.

Luke turned his head to see what caught my attention, and his back stiffened. She wasn't smiling, but she didn't look like a she was prepared for battle, either.

"Hi there, big brother," she said, as she approached. "Looks like we were both fooled."

They embraced, and I could readily see that their bond was still intact. I decided to sneak off for a bit and give them some space to talk about Amber and Jett. I wandered over to my Scooby Gang and listened to Kit regale everyone with one of her patented Parkville adventures. She seemed to know every nook and cranny of this town, and there was always a new tale to tell. Soon, Luke led Lana over by the hand to join us, I thought, but she gave him a quick goodbye peck on the cheek, instead.

"See you Sunday?" she said, and he nodded. "That includes you." She was looking directly at me, eyebrows raised. It was a statement, not a question.

"Um, yes," I said. "See you Sunday," and I smiled.

Maybe the ice was thawing, after all?

■ ■ ■

"Nervous?" Luke asked, as we pulled up to the Walcotts. "Don't be."

"I'm not," I lied, unconvincingly. "How often are we expected at these brunches?"

"Once a month, give or take," he said, "depending on everyone's availability. Sometimes Lana is busy with Amber, but I'm guessing that will happen a lot less, now."

"I still can't believe Amber went through all of that…" I said, not finishing.

"Just for me?" he laughed.

"Seriously, right? If she only knew how much you hogged the entire bed."

"Hey, I told you to just tap me. I'll move. And you snore, by the way." He poked me.

"I *do* tap you," I said. "But if I snore, you can just continue to ignore me, okay?"

"Deal."

Luke rang the doorbell and we could hear footsteps walking towards the door. Even though I was feeling uneasy about all of this, I was kind of looking forward to one of Rosa's warm hugs.

"Come on in, y'all. Welcome," Lana said, as she opened the door.

I was surprised to see her and not Rosa greeting us. She reached out and gave Luke a hug and a peck on the cheek. She then looked at me and we both mutually froze for a second, unsure of whether to shake hands or just nod and smile. She leaned over gingerly and gave me a half hug with one arm, not quite as listless as I imagined it would be, but not yet a full-fledged embrace. At this point I was happy to take what I could get. It was a start.

"Michael and Bammy are already here," she said. "It's such a lovely spring day, Daddy suggested we have lunch out on the gazebo. Why don't y'all go out and join them and I'll see if Rosa needs any help in the kitchen?"

"See you there," said Luke, then he guided me through the long hallway towards the veranda. We stepped out onto the covered porch and immediately Red spotted us from the gazebo. He held his hand up, with a small wave hello. Bammy and Michael were seated opposite him, already enjoying a cocktail. We walked down the stairs and across the manicured lawn as the sun's rays smiled down on us.

"Welcome, welcome," said Red, not rising, but directing us to two empty chairs, instead. "Rosa has prepared a nice pitcher of sweet tea. Careful. She went a little heavy on the vodka for my taste, today. I think she's planning on getting us all a little lubricated."

"Vodka and sweet tea," I said, happily. "Now you're talking my language."

"Well, then," said Red, "I think you will fit in just fine 'round here. Just fine."

19

ONCE MORE, WITH FEELING

Everyone got the memo this time, and classes were in full swing on Monday.

It was a fantastic feeling to pull up to the school knowing that the CCCP would not be waiting to greet me with a morning tirade and fresh picket signs. Actually, I was going to miss the attention, just a little. Kidding. I was so grateful and relieved that the whole ordeal was over.

Well, almost over. There was still a small gaggle of local reporters trying to drag out the story. We didn't want to feed the machine anymore, so we just walked past them without commenting.

Luke and I held hands as we approached the school entrance, then (bravely) gave each other a quick kiss on the cheek before we went our separate ways. If anyone noticed, they didn't say anything, positive or negative. It felt so good to be just under the radar, again. For now. Here's hoping we could continue this way, without any further drama.

"Good morning, Miss Mabel," I said, as I entered the office. She barely looked up as I placed a fresh cup of coffee on her desk. I lingered for a moment, smiling.

"What are you expecting, Derek?" she asked. "A parade?"

"Nice to see some things haven't changed," I remarked. "I missed you, too, Miss Mabel. But you can't fool everyone. I know there's a story in there just dying to get out."

"Well, you keep buttering me up and we'll see about that someday," she said, all the while typing away at her computer.

"Thanks for the assist," I said to her, quietly. "You really saved our butts, you know that?"

"Well, somebody had to," she sighed.

I walked down the hall to check on Bammy before heading to my first period class. She was on the phone as I stood in the doorframe to her office.

"Yes, Mrs. Carter. As long as Chip attends the rest of the year and passes English, there should be no problems. No, ma'am. No, ma'am. Nobody is being punished for the walkout. Yes, ma'am. Indeed. Yes, it was fair. Yes, I understand. Well, we're all just respecting our differences. Yes, ma'am. Of course. I'll have Miss Mabel send that transcript right off to you as soon as the last day of school has ended. Yes, ma'am. You, too. Good day."

She put the phone receiver down and gave me that *just shoot me* look. "Please tell me you topped this coffee off with a healthy dosage from Miss Mabel's secret stash?" she asked, as I handed her a cup.

"How'd you know about that?" I asked.

"Oh, please," she said, taking her first careful sip. "That woman doesn't say much, but when she does, you can smell when she's happier than she ought to be."

"How's Mrs. Carter?" I joked, changing the subject. Mabel saved my ass. The last thing I wanted to do was cause her any grief.

"It's been a pretty steady parade of calls this morning. We put out a bulletin that none of the students would be punished for missing classes last week, but the parents are still concerned. They just want to make sure their kids are still on their approved career trajectories."

"If I ever have a kid I'll just be happy if he or she gets out of high school alive. There's way too much pressure in this place," I said.

"Kids just need good role models and some motivation and they can do anything."

"I guess good role models are in short supply these days?" I asked.

"Well, there are a few of us. You and Luke are good people. And there's always someone you can help out. Take Jett, for example? He could definitely use some positive guidance. And if you two were to ever think about having kids, you could certainly practice on him. Just a thought."

I glared at her, not because I disagreed, but because she was right. Deep inside, there was probably a decent kid hiding in there. But would Luke or I have the patience to help find him? And why was it up to us? It's not Luke's fault that Amber lost the Mother of the Year Award.

The warning bell rang for first period.

"Lunch later?" I asked. "Cochon's?"

"You got it," she said. "See you in the parking lot at 12. I'll drive!"

I had five minutes to get to my own class, so I sped on out the door, past the swinging office gate and up the main stairwell.

As I entered the classroom, my students were still milling about, chatting and laughing. I closed the door behind me and they reacted to the sound by moving towards their seats and quieting down, until a serene silence took over the room. Jett was seated in his usual spot, blankly looking ahead and my theatre students were sitting on their side of the room, just like always. The great divide. One week ago seemed like an eternity, suddenly.

I did a quick roll call, and everyone was present. The mood was strangely tense. It was as if no one knew what to say or how to get back to where we were. Come on guys, it's over! Someone had to crack the ice. It may as well be me, right?

"So," I started, "did I miss anything interesting?"

There was a prolonged moment of silence, followed by a thunderous outburst of laughter from Jett. Pretty soon the other students joined in. We were off to a loud start, but I was pretty sure that Principal Talbot wouldn't mind our noise level today.

■ ■ ■

The next few weeks flew by. Because of the walkout, the school year had been extended one extra week in June, but most of the seniors only needed to pass English for that last necessary credit before they moved on to their new universities. Basically, everyone's attention span was reset to zero, and even the teachers considered the end of this semester a wash. We were just trying to squeeze as much out of the last few weeks as we could, knowing that our only goal was to ensure that the doors stayed open, as they should. Keeping the school board happy meant keeping the kids in their seats, and we were all doing our part.

I was grateful that my Theatre Arts Club had worked on *The Crucible* on their own during their week off. It was easy enough for us to get right back on track again with rehearsals, and before we knew it, tech week was upon us. Having spent so many hours as a student toiling away on the stage under the direction of my predecessor, Miss B., it still felt a bit strange that I was now cast in the role of faculty advisor, myself. I was having a great time teaching, and my students were really like my own kids. Well, to be honest, they were the perfect kids, because I only had them from 8am to 3:30pm, and then someone else took over. Regardless, it had been an incredibly rewarding, albeit challenging, year, but as it was quickly coming to a close, I felt the need to analyze my choices, again. Was this really where I wanted to be? I didn't mean Parkville, and I certainly wasn't questioning my relationship with Luke, my family or my Scooby Gang. However, the struggles we had just endured over a simple kiss… well, I was starting to wonder if I really wanted to remain in a place that did not want me for who I truly am.

It was almost Opening Night, and I had spent four very long nights after school running lighting cues and rehearsing with the students in the auditorium. Tech weeks are always difficult, but our efforts were really starting to come together. They were definitely going to put on a good show.

"All right y'all, gather 'round," I called out to the cast and crew on Thursday night. "Listen, I just want to say how proud I am of all of you. You guys are the ones who pulled this together, and it wasn't easy. I changed my mind about which play we were doing, then there was the walk-out, all the drama. But y'all stayed focused, and it shows. You're gonna do great tomorrow, no doubt about it. Okay!" I clapped my hands together. "Call time tomorrow is 6pm, and then curtain is at 8. Now go home tonight and get a good night's rest! See you tomorrow."

I could barely stay focused the next day at school. I knew the kids would do a great job, but I had the jitters, anyway. I always get a little nervous before a show, but my Spidey sense was in overdrive. Something was up, but at least I was certain that my ex-boyfriend David wasn't going to show up tonight with flowers, like last semester. Right?

Mom asked me to swing by her house for a quick chat before the show. Luke was coaching track practice after school, so he planned on meeting me at the auditorium, later. I pulled Willie into the driveway, and Johnny's car was there, as well as Uncle Barry's. Hail, hail the gang's all here!

I walked in the side door and threw my keys in the cigar box on the table, but the three of them barely registered my presence, they were so quiet. Mom and Johnny were seated together on the couch, staring ahead, and Barry was in his usual place in the overstuffed chair, legs up on the ottoman. But no one was smiling.

"What's up?" I asked, slowly stepping towards them. "Did somebody die?" I asked, half jokingly. Nobody answered me.

"Wait. No, really?" I asked, again. "I was kidding. But, we don't have anybody else. It's just us. What's going on?"

"Oh, sweetie," my mom said, looking up at me, "it's nothing bad, at all. It's good, really. I think we're all just trying to soak it in."

"Y'all are scaring me," I said, nervously.

"Sit down, honey," she said. "Your dad and I want to talk to you."

"Okay," I mumbled, pulling up a chair from beside the couch. "Just go for it. No sugar coating, all right? Is it cancer?" I didn't whisper it, like we do in the South. By now I was too scared to play any more of these silly games.

She smiled and reached out for Johnny's hand. "*No*, Derek, nothing like that, at all! I told you it was good. It's just a change, that's all. It will take a bit of adjusting, for all of us." She paused, then looked at Johnny, who was suddenly beaming. "It's about your dad and me. We've decided to get back together. I'm moving to the farmhouse with him. We're giving it another shot, sweetie."

"Really?" I said. "That's it?" They nodded. "That's awesome! Why's everybody so freaked out?"

"You're okay with this?" asked Johnny. "Because I love her. I do. I'm not the same man I was years ago, and your mom can see that." He was trying to convince me, but it was unnecessary. I had recognized the change in Mom since his return.

"I think our cupboards can see that," I said. "They've never been filled with so many organic foods."

"So, you're cool with this? Well, that takes a load off my mind," he said, relieved. "It took a bit to get everybody on board, but I want you both to know, we're going to make this work, this time. Really."

"You'd better," said Barry, reaching his hand out for the cocktail that was sitting on the table by his side. "Because if you're moving all these dusty treasures out of this house, then there's no turning back, understand? I can finally make the bachelor palace of my dreams! I'm thinking I may need a hot tub in the back. I'm going to need to speak to your friend Tommy, Derek. He does renovations, right? It's about time I found a little fun of my own, don't you think?" He put the drink to his lips and I couldn't help but notice the shiny bling on his wrist.

"Something new?" I asked, nodding towards the sparkling links.

"Oh, this?" he giggled, arm extended. "Just a little peace offering. Diamonds *are* a girl's best friend after all, Dolly."

■ ■ ■

The Crucible went off without a hitch. Fortunately, the parallels between the Salem witch trials of the 17th century and Parkville's CCCP were lost on most of the parents and students who filled the auditorium, but I was actually relieved that I wasn't singled out (again) for doing anything scandalous. It was nice not to be noticed, for a change.

Thankfully my ex did not show up with flowers tonight, however I was surrounded by all my friends and loved ones when I came out into the auditorium after the curtain call. We had really become an extended family after the ordeals of the last few months, and with the addition of Johnny and Michael, we were growing larger every day. Luke held my hand, subtly, as if nothing else mattered in the world, but there was still a bit of underlying tension in the room. It was hard to shake that feeling that we were "misbehaving" on school grounds, as we had promised not to do.

"Waddya say we get out of here and celebrate?" I asked, ready to move.

"The Firelight!" said Kit, gleefully, hands raised in the air. She was happier than a kid who had just been offered extra candy on Halloween. Shawn pulled her close and couldn't suppress his laughter. Dating Kit was certainly going to keep him young.

Mom, Johnny and Barry bowed out, as expected. They were going to start packing up Mom's things over the weekend. The rest of us took off in our various cars and made our way downtown towards the dive bar we liked to treat as our home away from home. We took over the big circular booth, filling the table top with beers and shots of whiskey. Kit had somehow convinced the bartender to make her a pitcher of Cosmopolitans, even though this really wasn't that kind of a bar. She truly was magical. She held her martini glass high, the soft pink liquid reflecting the light from the dusty swinging lamp above us.

"To Derek!" she said. "You went through a shit storm, baby, but you came out shining like a star!"

We all laughed and clinked our glasses. "Well, the school year's not over yet. Just two more weeks to go. No telling what will happen," I said.

"Please don't jinx us, babe," said Luke, lifting his arm and putting it around my shoulder, pulling me close. "I could use some down time with a little less drama, if you know what I mean?"

"Yeah, it must really suck getting a surprise new brother," said Michael, smiling slyly.

"Oh, you have no idea," said Luke, winking. They were growing closer by the day, bonding over sports and filling each other in on their childhoods and family dynamics. Michael was working closely with Red now, which freed Luke up from some of the obligations and guilt he had felt when he decided not to enter the family business.

And Bammy? She had her man, finally, and he was definitely the kind of guy she could bring home to her mom. "Well, not only did you get a new brother, but Derek and I now get Walcott family brunches every month, as a bonus."

"*Oooh!* Do tell!" said Meredith, her eyes shining. "I've always wondered what the inside of that big house looks like."

"Well, now that my job is done at Amber's place, maybe Red has some carpentry work he'd like done?" asked Tommy, testing the waters. "Then we can take a look?"

"Y'all don't need to do any work to come by the house," said Luke. "I'll tell Rosa we'd like to have a get together with all our friends. She'll love it."

"And you will all love Rosa's drinks!" I assured them. "Her goal is to get everyone toasted, every time."

"*My. Kinda. Girl!*" said Kit, smiling wildly.

"I hope I'm invited?" said a voice behind us, quietly. We all turned to look, but I knew who it was before I had even caught sight of her.

"If that's okay, of course?" she asked again, defensively. Her arms were folded across her chest, one forearm looped through yet another enormous, expensive leather bag.

"Of course it's okay, Lana," said Luke, standing up to greet his sister and give her a hug. "Don't be silly. You know everyone, right?"

"Yes, I think so," she half-whispered, feigning a smile. "Though I probably haven't made the best impression, lately. But heck, we all make mistakes, right?" She was nervous. This was a side of her I hadn't seen before.

"Oh, *hell* no," I said. Everyone looked at me, stunned. Luke's brow furrowed, and I realized I'd better rescue my joke, but quickly. "Everybody knows *I'm* perfect, right?"

"Well, at least my brother seems to think so," said Lana, not skipping a beat. "But then again, he used to eat dog food when we were kids, so there's no accounting for taste." Zing!

"*Snap!* I like her!" said Kit. "You can sit next to me! Would you like a Cosmopolitan? Shawn, baby, go get us an extra martini glass." Kit pushed Shawn with two hands to make some room and fetch some extra glasses. We all readjusted, adding Lana to the mix.

"I only did that once!" said Luke, turning to me. "It was a dare, babe, I promise."

"Well, if you need me to pick up some Milk-Bone dog treats from the store next time, just put them on the list, okay? Your teeth *are* awfully white."

"See what you've done, Lana?" he said, poking his sister in the ribs.

"Yeah, see what you've done?" I added, smiling. "You've made yourself fit in." She eyed me, warily. It was going to be tough, but I was determined to make her smile. Shawn came back from the bar with a glass for her and Kit poured Lana a pink hued cocktail.

"To family?" I said, raising my glass.

"To family!" they all responded.

We were still laughing and drinking when closing time snuck up on us.

20

DUKE

Mom, Johnny and Barry spent the whole next week packing up the treasures she had collected over the years. I don't think Johnny realized what he was getting into when he asked her to move in, but the more they packed, the more he understood, and the more he sweated. His California lifestyle had led him to a simpler way of living, with fewer material goods to weigh him down. Now he was reversing course. Surprise, Johnny! Mom likes her stuff. A lot.

The more they packed, the happier Barry became. He had been rather concerned when he found out that Mom was dating Johnny again, and definitely a bit unhappy when she first told him privately that she was planning to move out. It wasn't so much about Johnny, he realized, but more that he was sure he would feel that loneliness creep back into his life, again. When Janey died, he had sold his own house and moved in with Mom, hoping for a fresh start and an escape from the memories. But I could tell he always felt like a visitor at this house, and suddenly he was relishing the thought of really making the place his own.

"You know I love you, Audrey," he said as he surveyed his new surroundings, "but I cannot wait to exile that awful wallpaper in the dining room to one of the nine circles of Hell."

"I love that wallpaper!" she cried.

"Too bad, darling. It's atrocious, and now it's *out*, like me!"

She frowned, but he was enjoying his new freedom and ready to make his mark. It was really amazing to watch his transformation. And he had been serious about the hot tub. Tommy was already putting a proposal together for him.

I helped out when I could after school, but we were all pretty busy tying up the loose ends around campus. Prom was coming up this weekend, and Luke and I had offered to serve as chaperones, along with Bammy, Miss Mabel and some of our other colleagues.

"Got your prom dress picked out, Miss Mabel?" I asked, as I placed a freshly purchased cup of coffee on her desk.

"Don't you tease me, Derek Walter," she said, not looking up. "I may not be a spring chicken, but I got plenty of spring in my step."

"Oh, no doubts about that, Miss Mabel," I said, smiling. "Save a dance for me?"

"I'll check my dance card," she mumbled. "If you can keep up with me, that is?"

"Challenge accepted! See you Saturday night."

The only news around the school was prom news. It was officially the only acceptable topic in class, in the hallways, at lunch, and even in the teachers' lounge. We were all reliving our pasts vicariously through our students. Well, some of us, but not all.

"What was the name of that guy you went to prom with, Bammy?" I asked her over lunch at Cochon's. We were sitting on an old picnic bench in the parking lot, taking a break from the students and our fellow teachers. It was a beautiful spring day and the sun was shining intensely in the sky overhead. "I swear I can't remember. I'm getting old."

"Which one?" she asked, looking at me oh-so-innocently as she took another sip of her diet soda.

"Seriously?" I said, putting my fork down and giving her the eye. "Do you need to remind me that you were never without a date all four years in high school? Just answer the question." Luke laughed a bit and kept focusing on his barbecue plate. He knew better than to step into this one.

"Let's see," she started. "Freshman year it was Kirby Pettit. We called him 'Dirty Kirby,' remember? Trust me, he earned that reputation. After I dumped him I started dating Parker Bingham. He lasted two years, actually. I used to practice writing 'Bammy Bingham' on all my notebooks. I really thought we were going to get married. He kinda broke my heart, truth be known, but that was all for the best. He runs a lawn maintenance company now, and I'm allergic to grass. It would have never worked out. Senior year, that was Travis Wyatt. Yep. He was special. So handsome. We had the best time at the prom, and everything would have been all fairy tale perfect, except he snuck a bottle of peach schnapps into the dance and he got way too drunk. By the time we ended up back at the hotel room he had rented, he could barely walk. The front desk clerk had to help us to our room. I look back on that and wonder why on Earth he even helped us at all. Times were different, I guess. Anyway, Travis kinda reanimated when we threw him on the bed. The hotel guy left the room and Travis started climbing all over me, thinking he was going to get some. I gave him a good punch in the gut, and that's when he puked all over the place. It was awful. I couldn't wait to get out of there."

"Oh, my god! Yes! Travis Wyatt. How could I forget that one? He was a real winner," I said.

"He played football with me," said Luke, looking up from his barbecue. "He threw up a lot on the field, too. He never could take a hit."

"Okay, okay," I said, turning to my boyfriend. "Enough about vomit. Luke? We don't really have to ask you, do we? Amber, right?"

"Yep," he said. "All four years. Amber Winthrop. We had some good times together, actually."

"Well, you would have had more fun with me," I teased. "I can guarantee that."

"I wasn't ready for you, then. But I have no doubt you're right." He leaned over and placed a wet, sloppy, honey barbecue covered kiss on my cheek.

"You only went to prom our senior year, right Derek?" asked Bammy. "With that new girl. What was her name?"

"Amy Carter," I mumbled.

"The president's daughter?" said Luke.

"Yes, Luke, the daughter of the president of the United States just happened to be in Parkville and her only wish was to go to prom with a closeted gay teenager," I deadpanned. "Her name was Amy Carter, and she hated it. She only went to our school for the last few months of our senior year. Her dad got transferred here for work, or something. I can't remember. Anyway, she didn't really know anybody and I had crushes on all the wrong people, so yeah... I asked the new girl. I figured I could at least get a prom picture, like all the other kids. I just wanted to fit in and do the stuff that everyone else was doing."

"Did you have fun, at least?" he asked.

"Not really," I said. "We had an overpriced dinner that I could barely afford, then we hung out behind the school, sneaking drinks like everybody else. I don't even think we danced that much. We had our picture taken as soon as we got to the dance and that was pretty much it. She smoked, so she kept disappearing. I don't even remember taking her home. She must have bummed a ride with someone else. I can't remember any more details. I think I blocked it all out."

Luke looked at me, sadly. "Babe, we gotta fix this this." He wiped his mouth, placed his napkin on the table and turned, extricating one of his legs from the picnic bench and readjusting himself to face me. He took both of my hands in his and looked straight at me, into my eyes.

"Derek Walter, will you go to prom with me?"

"Why, I'd be delighted to, Luke Walcott," I said, smiling a huge grin. "But I have to be home by midnight, otherwise my boyfriend will suspect I'm up to something."

"It's a date then," he said, turning on the bench again. "I'll pick you up at 7 o'clock."

"I expect a flower for my lapel," I instructed him.

"As you wish, handsome," he said.

Bammy put her soda can down with a dramatic bang. "Y'all make me sick. Seriously. But, I do love ya. And I want a picture."

■ ■ ■

"Derek! Are you ready, yet? Luke's gonna be here any minute and I want to get some pictures." Mom was yelling up the staircase as I was running back and forth from the bathroom to my bedroom and back again, checking my outfit and my hair, as if it could possibly change that much in the thirty seconds since I last checked it. I was undeniably nervous, and it was silly, but here I was, prepping for the prom I never had with the guy I always wanted. I took a deep breath and closed my bedroom door behind me. In a sense, I felt like I was a high school senior again, and I had a do-over. Dreams do come true, after all?

I collected myself and started walking down the stairs. Mom and Johnny were waiting for me, and Barry practically had tears forming in his eyes. "Seriously, y'all?" I said. "It's a dance. I'm way too old for this to mean anything."

"Are you kidding me?" said Johnny. "I missed all of this. I'm loving every minute of it. Now get over here and let me take a picture of you and your mom." He pulled his phone out and started snapping away; me, mom and son, uncle and nephew, dad and son, and every other combination possible. We heard a car pull up in the driveway and I started towards the door.

"Don't you dare!" said my mom. "You wait until your gentleman caller rings that doorbell. Do not appear over eager. Have I not taught you anything?"

"Yes ma'am," I laughed, as I stood waiting in the living room, my hands behind my back.

The bell rang and Barry made a move towards the door, but then hesitated and glanced towards Johnny. It was a nice gesture on his part. Looks like you're up, Dad.

"Good evening, sir," said Luke, as Johnny opened the door. "I'm here to escort Derek to the prom. Is he ready?" So formal! Pansy, Red and Rosa did, indeed, raise him well.

"Come on in, Luke," said Dad. "His mom and I are kind of excited. We're going to need a few pictures, if you don't mind?"

"Not at all, sir." He stepped through the doorframe and my heart skipped a bit. I thought I had seen him in every possible way, but the truth was, I was used to Luke in a tight t-shirt and blue jeans or coach shorts. To see him dressed up in a dark navy suit, walking through my mother's door to escort me to a dance, well, honestly, that moment pretty much broke me. Barry had already given up all pretenses of keeping it together, and I almost lost it watching the tears roll down my proud uncle's face. They were happy tears, but I understood.

Luke walked over to me and kissed me lightly on the cheek, his hand at the small of my back. "You look great," he said, admiring my suit. "I hope this will do?" He opened the clear plastic container and offered me a red rose for my lapel. "Audrey, I may need some help with this," he said, nervously. Were his hands shaking?

"Oh, give me that!" said Barry. "I want to be part of this. It's not everyday I get to see two handsome men in suits, holding hands. It's mostly sequins and feathers on my side of town." He took the flower from Luke's hands and pinned it expertly on my lapel. "There, Dolly. Beautiful. I'm so happy for you," he whispered, looking directly into my eyes.

"All right, gents," said Johnny. "Let's take some pictures!"

Mom suggested we step outside to get some classic prom poses in the front yard, and we all agreed that would be fun. I was a bit overwhelmed by the family whirlwind, but I was having a blast. I wasn't prepared, however, for what we saw in the driveway. In place of the Jeep that I expected, there was a black stretch limousine!

"Holy shit!" I exclaimed. "Seriously?"

"Seriously," he nodded. "You missed out on too many things. Tonight you're getting the full experience."

"You really are the best, you know that?"

"Well, why don't you hold off on the praise until the night is over?" he smiled. "We'll see how you feel, then."

Mom, Johnny and Barry then took an endless stream of pictures and videos, until we practically had to push them away. We didn't want to be late for our own party. We walked over to the limousine and the handsome young driver opened the door for us. I saw him wink at Barry as we slid inside. Old friend? Or possibly new? I'd have to get the scoop on that, later. Right now we were ready to party!

Luke held my hand the entire way to the school. We rode in silence, just smiling. So many things had happened in the last year since I had returned home, that words didn't seem capable of covering it all. I just knew that the hand I held in my own meant so much more to me than any words could ever express.

The gymnasium was decked out in the school colors of blue and gold. Go Commodores! Streamers and balloons filled the room, and the space was filling up quickly with students. We spotted Bammy and Michael across the room by the punch bowl and began to make our way through the crowd to greet them.

"You look beautiful!" I said to her, as I gave her a hug. Bammy always could pull off a Southern debutante dress with style. Michael looked handsome in his dark grey suit, and I could see that the Walcott genes had played out in his favor. Those boys do clean up well.

"And y'all are as handsome as ever! We're on punch bowl duty," she said, as she kissed me on the cheek. "Someone has to guard it all night. I don't want any of these girls to relive my peach schnapps nightmare, if you get my drift?"

"Hopefully there aren't any Travis Wyatt clones here tonight," I said.

"Well, I put y'all on dance floor duty," she said. "My treat. I figured you'd enjoy a few slow dances together. You deserve it after this semester. Might be nice?"

"Thanks, Bammy," said Luke. He turned to me and held out his hand and said, "May I have this dance, sir?"

I hesitated. "Not just yet, if you don't mind. Trust me, you're all I want right now, but I made a promise I need to keep. Don't be jealous, okay?"

He looked at me quizzically, but nodded. I had spotted Miss Mabel across the room by the coat check, so I walked over in that direction. She was sitting on a metal fold out chair, watching the parade of boys and girls as they entered the room. I could only imagine what was on her mind.

"Has that dance card filled up yet, Miss Mabel?" I asked. "I hope you saved a spot for me."

Her knees were together, shifted to the side, legs crossed at the ankles. Her gloved hands were resting in her lap, and I imagined her in the same position many years ago, looking out onto the dance floor, unable to have the experience she was longing for in her heart.

"Now, you know I don't go that way," she said, looking up at me, staring into my eyes defiantly, no longer hiding what she knew I already knew. "But for you, Derek Walter, I'll make an exception."

She offered her hand and I helped her up, gently, as I led her towards the dance floor. A slow tempo song was playing, so I placed my right arm around her waist with my hand at the small of her back, my left arm raised and clasping her gloved hand, back straight. We swayed slowly to the music, a respectable distance between our bodies. I didn't really know what to say, or if I would ruin the moment by saying anything, at all. This was the most she had ever looked at me in the year since I had returned. She kept her emotions and thoughts closely guarded, and I didn't expect that to change tonight. Then her eyes broke contact with mine and drifted off into space.

"I loved her, you know? Your Aunt Janey," she said, acknowledging the relationship that had remained wholly unspoken between us. My face betrayed my thoughts for a moment and I couldn't help but smile, slightly. I knew better than to speak too much. If she was ready to say something, I didn't want her to stop.

"Yes, ma'am," I replied, quietly. "Barry told me you were close."

"Barry," she muttered. "He always was up in everybody else's business." My chest jumped with a few stifled laughs.

"But, he always treated her well," she continued. "That I can say. They knew what they had, that relationship. They had fun, too. Worked out best for everyone, it did. But she was mine, Janey. Ain't no doubt 'bout that." We continued to move softly to the music, her words growing stronger as she reminisced. "I was supposed to get married to Lamont Evans. Bet you didn't know that? Mama and Daddy arranged it. His family went to our church. But I fought them every step of the way. Headstrong. I made sure that boy knew I was a world of trouble. He hightailed it 'fore they could change his mind, again. That was fine by me. By the time I finished secretarial school, they stopped trying. They figured I'd die an old maid. My choice, though, that was. Too ornery, they said. But Janey didn't think so. I met her at the drug store, one day. She admired my hat and asked where I bought it. That was nice of her, taking that first step. She was a brave girl. Wasn't long before we were laughing up a storm in that drug store, all kinds of folks staring at us. She loved my fire, she said. It was unusual, back then, a black girl and white girl being best friends. Janey took some heat for that. No doubt. But she kept on. Never walked away from me, even when it got ugly. I was several years older than her, you know. Soon enough, people just got used to seeing us together. The old maid and the white girl. Haha!" She practically cackled. "They didn't know nothin'. It all worked out, though. She had her time with Barry and her time with me. It was necessary, you know. It's a different world you're living in, Derek Walter," she said, looking up at me, again. "You be happy for what you got. You and Luke. You be grateful. You think you had it hard this year, but you don't know nothing'. You don't know hard. You understand me?"

"Yes, ma'am, I do," I replied, standing still as the song changed and the tempo began to build.

"Now you get over there and dance with your man, you hear me?" she said, fiercely. "You go do what I couldn't. 'Cause we fought for that, in our own way. It just took too long for Janey and me to benefit from that battle. But you go claim what's yours. You got me? Now, go set me back down. But bring me a little plastic cup. I'm gonna need a little of my medicine to get through all this."

"Yes, ma'am," I smiled. "My pleasure." I walked her back over to her chair, then retrieved a plastic cup from the refreshments table and placed it in her hand as she reached for the flask inside the coat pocket she had draped over her chair.

"Go on. *Git*," she said with a nod of her head, and I was dismissed as quickly as I had been welcomed.

"Trying to make me jealous?" said Luke, as I sidled up beside him.

"Did it work?" I asked.

"Get over here," he said, as he pulled me into his arms and kissed me softly. "We're supposed to be monitoring the dance floor, remember?"

"Lead the way, Mr. Walcott," I demurred.

He took my hand and pulled me gently through the crowd as we made our way to the center of the dance floor. It was an uptempo song, so we didn't have to have that awkward discussion about who was leading. Jett and his date happened to be dancing just to our left, next to Chip Carter and his girlfriend. Jett looked over at Luke and me and nodded. "Hey, Pops!" he jeered. "Lookin' good. You, too, *Mr. Derek*." He and Chip exchanged high fives over their dates' heads. That kid really was a piece of work, but maybe Bammy was right. He just needed a good role model. Perhaps Luke and I could step up, in some way, after all? I don't know. I had my mentors over the years. Maybe that's all he needed, too?

It was amazing how quickly this had all escalated: the CCCP, the walkout, the turmoil. But just as soon as it was over, it was over. No one wanted to keep dredging up the past, and we were back to quietly ignoring our differences, pretending that they weren't there to begin with. A few kids snickered at us, but overall, no one seemed to care much. Occasionally a wolf whistle would ring out through the air, directed our way. I always wondered, didn't the straight guy who did that realize he was the one flirting with *us*? No, they just ignore that aspect of the equation. It's uncomfortable. But I didn't *want* to ignore everything. I wanted to be me, again, without the smoke and mirrors and self-awareness, especially after my conversation with Miss Mabel. Too many people fought too hard for too many years for us to accept a life in the shadows as second-class citizens. Activist me was starting to argue with pacifist me, but perhaps I should hold off on that? Right now I just wanted to dance.

The DJ switched gears again and the opening strains of *Time After Time* by Cyndi Lauper started playing. Luke looked into my eyes and I could sense a change in his demeanor.

"Babe?" I asked. "What's up? Are you okay?"

"Never better," he answered, "but I have something to ask you." He stepped back, holding both of my hands in his, then bent down on one knee. I froze. A circle of students formed around us, all of them slowing down to watch, some of them making faces, others just too shocked to believe it. Cell phones suddenly appeared all around us, snapping pictures and videos. I could see Jett and Chip smirking out of the corner of my eye. My heart started racing. Luke, no. No, no, no! We are definitely not ready for this. How can I stop him from...

"Derek?" he spoke, looking up at me from his bent knee position. "Will you..."

■ ■ ■

We woke up the very next morning and headed over to Red's for the monthly Walcott Brunch, except today it was planned as a get together for our extended family and friends. Luke told me that Rosa usually liked taking care of everything by herself, but since the group was so large today, she brought in some help from Lloyd's, the go-to caterer for Parkville's elite. She was still in charge, there was no doubt about that, but now she had a small army of attractive ladies and strapping young men in crisp white tuxedo shirts and black trousers running back and forth from the kitchen, carrying silver trays arranged with fancy hors d'oeuvres. Rosa had decided on a Southern theme for the day, with just a hint of a Mexican twist. There were mini cheese biscuits with a slice of ham and jalapeño jam, fried shrimp on wooden skewers with a picante dipping sauce, and amazingly tasty mini crab cakes. A full buffet was set up not far from the gazebo, with a chef carving a roast beef. The bar was set up on the veranda, featuring an assortment of beers, spirits and, of course, micheladas and margaritas. Lloyd Barton stood at the edge of the crowd, surveying his handiwork, snapping his fingers and firing off commands to his staff as they passed him. He was getting on in years, but his services were still in high demand.

"Very nice, Lloyd, as always," I heard Red say, as Luke and I arrived on the veranda. "Rosa is very pleased."

"Well, thank you kindly, Red," he responded. "I know Rosa has a firm command over this house, but it's always a pleasure when she relinquishes it just a little bit to our team. We'll get back to work, now. See you at the club, later this week? I hear Belle's worked out a new number that's sure to cause a ruckus. At least, from what she says!" They chuckled together, shook hands and parted. Well, Lloyd Barton, that wasn't much of a surprise revelation. It seemed most of Parkville's leading men were members of the Bears' Club. I guess Luke and I were too young, and too out, to get invited to that party.

"Welcome, gentleman," said Red, as he turned to greet us. "Rosa is running around here somewhere, but most of your friends have already arrived. Can I interest you in a cocktail?"

"Yes, sir," said Luke. "I'll get those." He walked over to the bartender and ordered a michelada for himself and a Bloody Mary for me.

"Things have settled down, I see," said Red to me, while Luke was at the bar. "That is good. I was not too fond of all the attention, as you may have surmised."

"Yes, sir," I nodded. "We're pretty happy that it's all over, too. And Michael seems to be settling in well, wouldn't you say?" I spotted him down at the gazebo with Bammy, drink in hand, caught up in a lively conversation with Kit and Shawn. Tommy and Meredith were holding hands, taking a stroll around the garden. He was pointing towards the horizon at some unknown landmark off in the distance.

"Michael is a fine boy," said Red. "I made an error in judgment many years ago, and I am grateful that he has seen fit to forgive me. He and Rosa, both. Family ties are very important to me, as you well know."

"Well, he's told us all that he's really enjoying working with you," I said. "Bammy said he's never been happier." Luke rejoined us, handed me my drink and placed one arm securely around my waist. Was he protecting me from Red? Old habits, I suppose, but I didn't think it was necessary, anymore. Nonetheless, I enjoyed the feeling of security.

"That was not the only error I have made in my lifetime," he continued. "Luke, your mother may not have outwardly approved of your recent revelations, but there is one thing that is certain in my mind. She may not have been the best at expressing her emotions, however she did indeed love you and your sister, and her only goal was to see you two happy. I'm sure, with time, she would have come to respect your relationship, as Rosa and I have. You may not believe me, but she would have taken a liking to you, Derek. Posy connected well with those few in our midst who have a little something extra hidden behind their eyes, as you do. She did love her secrets." He smiled, to himself.

Before we could respond, Rosa opened the door from inside the house. "*Mi amor*? We have more guests." Smiling, she held out her hand as Mom, Johnny and Barry stepped out onto the veranda.

"Why, Audrey Walter! My stars, you do *not* seem to age," said Red, as he took my mom's hands and kissed her cheek.

"Oh, Red, you sweet talker," she responded. "Some things just improve with time. You remember my husband, Johnny?"

"Yes, of course. A pleasure to see you, again," he said, grasping his hand for a firm shake. "It has been some years. Luke and Derek did tell me you have returned from California. Welcome."

"I don't age either, Red," Barry interjected, "but my secret's not so much of a secret. I'm just pickled. Vodka does *wonders*! But enough with our beauty secrets and social graces, join me for a cocktail? I know this is a social affair, but I have a few Bears' Club items I'd like to bring up, if that's all right? I'd like to discuss this 'rezoning' issue that Mayor Bellman is taking on as his big fight. I think our friend Belle hasn't really thought this thing through. What say you and I put our heads together to put a kibosh on that, hmmm? Before some rather damaging information gets out, if you know what I mean?"

"I'd say I agree with you wholeheartedly, my friend," said Red, smiling. "No sense stirring up any more nonsense than we need to, right?" They wandered away together, making their plan to bring Belle back down to size. They were an odd pair, but I could see the affection they shared for one another. I'd have to fill Luke in on that story, one day. Maybe.

"Why don't you all grab a drink and join us down at the gazebo?" said Luke to my family, then took my hand as we walked down the steps and onto the well manicured lawn.

"Did you ever in your life imagine a day like this?" I asked him, as we walked towards the gazebo. "Your family and mine, cocktails, Michael, all of our friends?"

"It's a lot to take in," he said. "But, no, not really. It's kind of crazy."

"Should we tell them?" I asked.

"Of course," he said, stopping in the grass. "It's the perfect day. Everyone's here. I want to scream it at the top of my lungs."

"You don't think it's too fast?"

"Babe, Tarzan always gets his love, right?" he said, smiling.

"And the greyhound keeps his eye on the prize," I said as I kissed him.

"And the sister always shows up to spoil the mood," said Lana, just behind us. When did she get here? We turned to look at her walking towards us, just a few steps away. And boy, did she ever bring a mood spoiler, standing right behind her.

"I like to keep y'all on your toes," she said, as a way of excusing herself before reaching over to give Luke a kiss on the cheek, then, surprisingly, directing an air kiss towards me, several inches from the landing zone.

"Before y'all freak out, let me say something," she started. "We've all made mistakes, so let's not pretend that we're all perfect. Casting stones hasn't worked out for *any* of us, in either direction. I think we all learned that. Beside, she's been my best friend since we were kids, and that's not changing, no matter what. Amber? Would you like to add anything?" she asked.

Amber stepped out from behind Lana, a demure but defiant smile on her face. She looked perfectly put together, as always, the picture perfect Southern belle.

"Luke," was the only word she uttered.

"Amber," he said, holding my hand tighter, his jaw clenching.

"Oh, Luke," she purred, "let's just put all this silly nonsense behind us, all right?" Even now she thought she could just smile and get away with everything. That may have worked in the past, but no longer.

"Well, that's not as easy as it sounds, Amber," he said. "I get that you were pissed off, but… Jett? What the hell? That's seriously messed up, Amber."

"Well, yes," she said, casting her eyes down, then up, "I know. But what's a girl to do, Luke? So I made up a little story. A colorful fib. I wouldn't be the first woman who pulled a few tricks out of the bag to try and get a man, now would I? But defeat is defeat, and I accept it. I'm sorry for all the mess I caused. I *am*. Forgive me?" She batted her lashes and looked up at him. My god, she never does give up.

Luke looked at me for approval and I just sighed and shook my head. *Whatever. Let's just move on. No more bodies, okay?* He understood the look in my eyes.

"Apology accepted. But it'll be awhile before I can trust you, again," he warned.

Her smile beamed and she reached up and threw her arms around his neck, practically pushing me out of the way in the process.

"And," he added, "I expect you to be civil to Derek."

"Why, of course," she gushed, without even looking at me. "Now, introduce me to that new brother of yours? What's his name, again? Michael? Is he seeing anyone?" She grabbed his hand and practically pulled him up the gazebo steps. Watch out, Bammy. It seems Miss Amber has now set her sights on *your* man, instead. I guess she doesn't know that Bammy has a mean right hook. Personally, I couldn't wait for those fireworks.

"He's happy," said Lana, watching Luke and Amber climb the stairs. "I suppose we have you to blame for that." I knew she was teasing with her choice of words, and it made me smile. She was coming around.

"Well," I said, "if your mother and Rosa and you had not raised such an amazing Southern gentlemen, then he wouldn't have been in such high demand. So I suppose I can partially blame you for that."

She raised an eyebrow and smiled. "Come on," she said. "We'd better jump on up there before they suspect we're being too friendly with each other. No sense scaring everyone today."

"I agree." I held my arm out and she slipped her hand through the crook of my elbow.

We joined the Scooby Gang on the gazebo and began enjoying the glorious afternoon. Rosa, Red, Johnny, Mom and Barry joined us, and soon we were at maximum capacity. Rosa had the waiters refill our drinks and bring up platters of food, and the sounds of laughter and clinking ice cubes filled the air.

The afternoon grew richer with new family and new friends. My handsome Southern gentleman, of course, found the perfect moment to share our news. Luke stood at the end of the long table, opposite his father, and tapped his spoon along the side of his glass. *Clink, clink, clink.* "May I have everyone's attention?" he asked. The crowd grew quiet, and shifted their focus towards him. The wait staff had long since stepped to the side, obediently waiting for further instructions, their arms clasped behind their backs. Lloyd Barton had trained them well. The sun was starting to set on the horizon and the soft glow of the pink sky was upon us.

"Father, Rosa," he began, "thank you both so much for inviting all of us here today. It's been so nice to be surrounded by all of our family, new and old, as well as our friends. And since we all have you here, Derek and I would like to make a little announcement." Eyes shifted left to right and various hands placed their cocktails down in order to pay full attention.

"It was just under a year ago that Derek and I met, again," he began. "We knew each other in high school, but not really. It took a few years, and a few girlfriends," he glanced at Amber, "for us to realize what we could mean to each other, and we've spent the last few months really enjoying our time together, even if that meant standing up to an entire town. But that brought us closer together. We even went to the prom last night and had the kind of experience we couldn't have had in high school. Things change, and thankfully times do, as well, albeit slowly. We're getting there, though. I can feel it. Throughout all of this, Derek has been spending a lot of time at my place, and, well, we'd just like to make it a bit more official. It's really no big deal, but we just wanted to tell all y'all at once... We're moving in together!"

"Oh, my goodness!" exclaimed Bammy. "I'm *so* happy that cat's out of the bag! I couldn't that news in much longer, after we saw Luke get down on one knee at the dance last night. *Whew!*"

"Does that mean I have the entire house to myself, now?" said Barry, practically squealing with glee. "Tommy! We need to revisit those plans. I'm gonna need much more than just a hot tub!"

"Oh, sweetie," said Mom, holding my dad's hand. "We're so happy for you. Really!"

"Now, will you two be remaining in Luke's house, or will you be moving on to something better?" asked Red, always the developer.

"We haven't decided that, yet," I answered. "The only thing we're sure of is that we need a little vacation, after the last few months we've had."

"It's been quite a crazy year, hasn't it, babe?" said Luke, a gleam in his eye.

I smiled, happy knowing that I was about to move in with the man of my dreams. "Yes, Luke. It has definitely been wild."

ACKNOWLEDGEMENTS

When I published my first novel, *Home is a Fire*, I was unsure of how it would be received. To say I was overwhelmed by the positive reaction is an understatement. *The Fire Went Wild* is in your hands today because of the support of you, the readers, and for that I remain extremely grateful.

I have to thank my friend Jesse Summers for his help in editing the first draft. He reads without prejudice and is not afraid to tell me when I've gone too far, or not far enough.

Many wonderful friends volunteered to help me proofread the final manuscript. Thank you Karyn Adams, Eunice Chang, Cynthia Tady, Bethany Wright Tillman, Angie Vicars and Cheryl Turner Walker for reading again and again, pointing out typographical mistakes, and making clear and helpful suggestions to improve the text and the story. Any errors that remain are my own.

Thank you to Patrik Nerséus for collaborating on and producing the perfect cover art. Tack, min vän!

I would also like to thank my own personal Scooby Gang and my many wonderful friends around the world for their continued love and support. You know who you are.

I wanted to write a book about being gay in the South that my parents would enjoy reading. They loved it, and I feel as though I succeeded. Thank you for the life lessons, Linda, George and Mary.

And finally, thank you for the wonderful reviews on Amazon. I hope you like this one just as much, if not more. Love all!

ABOUT THE AUTHOR

Jordan Nasser left his dream job behind and took the opportunity to re-examine his life—an experience he highly recommends if you ever have the chance. A graduate of the University of Tennessee, he was raised in the South before mov-ing to New York City. He currently lives and writes in Stockholm, Sweden and Nice, France.

In his debut novel, *Home Is a Fire*, he drew upon his experiences as a gay man in the South. Outstanding reviews placed the book on the top ten rated LGBT fiction list. That story continues in his second novel, *The Fire Went Wild*.

www.jordannasser.com